ON THE RUN

TRISTAN BANCKS

ON THE
RUN

Margaret Ferguson Books
Farrar Straus Giroux • New York

Farrar Straus Giroux Books for Young Readers
175 Fifth Avenue, New York 10010

Printed in the United States of America by
R. R. Donnelley & Sons Company, Harrisonburg, Virginia
First U.S. edition, 2015
First published as *Two Wolves* in Australia by Random House Australia, 2014
1 3 5 7 9 10 8 6 4 2

mackids.com

Library of Congress Cataloging-in-Publication Data
Bancks, Tristan.
    On the run / Tristan Bancks. — First U.S. edition.
        pages cm
    First published in Australia by Random House Australia.
    Summary: Twelve-year-old Ben, who aspires to be a police officer, struggles to do the
right thing when his parents suddenly take him and his little sister "on vacation," and he
learns they took a large amount of money that was mistakenly deposited in their bank
account.
    ISBN 978-0-374-30153-8 (hardback)
    ISBN 978-0-374-30154-5 (e-book)
    [1. Criminals—Fiction.   2. Fugitives from justice—Fiction.   3. Fathers and sons—
Fiction.   4. Conduct of life—Fiction.   5. Family life—Australia—Fiction.   6. Australia—
Fiction.]   1. Title.

PZ7.B21766On 2015
[Fic]—dc23

                                                                    2014042435

Farrar Straus Giroux Books for Young Readers may be purchased for business or
promotional use. For information on bulk purchases please contact
Macmillan Corporate and Premium Sales Department at (800) 221-7945 x5442 or
by email at specialmarkets@macmillan.com.

For Amber Melody, Hux, and Luca. And for my grandmother Joan Bancks, who made everything better.

An old man tells his grandson one evening that there is a battle raging inside him, inside all of us. A terrible battle between two wolves. One wolf is bad—pride, envy, jealousy, greed. The other wolf is good—kindness, hope, love, truth. The child asks, "Which wolf will win?" The grandfather answers simply, "The one you feed."

—unknown origin

CONTENTS

ON THE RUN

COPS

"You keep runnin', you'll only go to jail tired," Ben Silver muttered.

He hit the "photo" button on his battered video camera and took another picture. He reached across his forest set and moved the legs on two small clay figures. Ben was eye-level with the action, peering between trees made from cellophane and toilet paper rolls and other found things.

He often mumbled his characters' lines as he shot a movie. Later, after he'd filmed everything, he would record the voices and add them to the pictures. He jotted the line in his brown leather notebook:

"You keep runnin', you'll only go to jail tired."

Ben took a bite from a microwaved jam doughnut. The jam was lava on his tongue, and he dropped the doughnut onto the plate. The floor around him was littered with clothes, shoes, a game console, two controllers, a bike wheel with no tire, a skateboard deck, school books, a jumbo-size bag of chips, and plates from long-forgotten afternoon snacks. Ben's favorite place. It was dark with the curtains closed, the only light coming from two lamps trained on the stop-motion set on his desk. Outside, his dog, Golden, barked like crazy.

Within the Woods was Ben's seventh stop-motion movie. In this scene a zombie thief named Dario Savini was running down a forest track with detective Ben Silver, Sydney's toughest cop, in pursuit. The detective was famous in Ben's movies for vanquishing werewolves, delinquent kids, and zombies.

There was a heavy knock.

"Hello. Police!"

Ben froze. He looked at his clay cop, but clay Ben just stood there on one foot, midstride, frozen.

Another heavy knock on the front door of the house. It didn't sound like Olive. She was in the backyard, playing pirates on the trampoline like she did every day after school.

Ben stood, walked quietly out of his bedroom, and tiptoed up the hall, heart keeping time with his footsteps. He moved through the living room to the front window and peered carefully from behind the dusty gray curtain.

It was raining and two police officers were huddled under the front awning. One fat. One skinny. Skinny was a lady. A couple of police cars were parked at the curb with two more cops standing under dark blue umbrellas next to one of the cars. Ben's body surged with excitement and fear. His dream was to become a detective once he had finished school.

Ben's little sister came in through the broken sliding back door, soaking wet. "Who is it?" Olive asked.

"Shhh," he whispered, raising a hand to tell her to stop, but Olive kept coming. She was small, white-blond, seven years old, one of the smartest kids Ben knew. She had already read *The Hobbit* by herself. For three weeks afterward she refused to speak unless people called her Gandalf.

The knock again. The lady officer walked past the window. Ben tucked himself in behind the curtain. The officer disappeared around the side of the house.

Olive shuffled in front of Ben. "Police!" she said in a too-loud voice. He placed his hand over her mouth. She peeled it off. "They're coming to get you for what you did."

Ben swallowed hard and moved slowly toward the door, wondering if Olive was right. Earlier, he had tied her to a chair in the bathroom and dangled a cockroach in front of her face, then dipped her toothbrush in the toilet. But it seemed like overkill for four police officers to be assigned to the case, even if it was a slow Tuesday at the station.

Ben opened the door just enough to peek out.

"Good afternoon," the policeman said.

"Hello," Ben said, squeezing his bottom lip.

The officer's hand rested on the butt of a gun nestled in the holster on his right hip. "Are your parents in?"

Ben shook his head, still looking at the officer through a six-inch gap between door and frame. Ben was pleased to see that being slightly overweight didn't stop you from getting into the force. Ben was slightly overweight himself. His nan said it was from the rotten dinners his parents fed him from the burger chain on the corner.

"Can you please tell me where they are?"

The murmur of the highway nearby and the low hum of the tall electrical tower in the empty block across the street filled the space between them.

"At work."

"You sure about that? We just need to have a quick word with them," the officer said, looking past Ben into the house.

"Mm-hm."

"Have you seen them this afternoon at all?"

Ben shook his head. "They're at work till four-thirty."

The officer flipped open a small notebook with a leather cover. "Ray Silver Car Wreckers, 137 Hope Street?"

He nodded.

The female officer returned. "No one around there," she said, posting a tight-lipped smile to Ben.

"Thank you for your help," said the man, and they turned to go.

"Do you want me to give them a message?" Ben asked.

"No, we'll catch up with them," said the lady officer.

They walked quickly into the rain and up the cracked concrete path, past the two rusted, doorless cars that sat in the long grass of the Silvers' front yard. Golden, a three-legged, sandy-colored kelpie mix, was tied up to one of the decaying cars. She barked excitedly at the officers as they climbed into their vehicles. The hum of the electrical tower was swallowed by the roar of the police cars as they sped off up Cooper Street.

Ben closed the door and stood there, not knowing what to do.

"Are they going to put you in jail?" Olive asked.

He went to the coffee table and picked up the phone, thoughts whirling. He put the phone down. He squeezed his bottom lip.

"What did they want?" Olive asked. "Did they say that dipping your sister's toothbrush in the toilet was a very bad thing to do?"

Ben picked the phone up again and dialed the number for the wreckers. The phone rang. And rang.

He was about to try his mum's cell phone when he heard tires skidding on the gravel out in front.

THE VACATION

"Cop!" Ben's dad called from the car. That was his nickname for Ben, because he asked so many questions.

Ben raced to the door and looked out. The Green Machine, his father's 1967 Valiant 770, was parked half on the road, half on the footpath. Painted flames licked the side and hood of the car.

"Let's go!" Dad shouted. Mum walked quickly toward the house, high heels clattering on the wet path. Olive squeezed past Ben and ran out into the rain to meet her.

"Grab a few things to do in the car," Mum said. "We've got a surprise for you."

"What is it? What is it?" Olive asked.

"If I told you it wouldn't be a surprise. Quick as you can."

Ben thought for a second and headed to his room. He grabbed his schoolbag, threw in his notebook and pencil and his camera. He scurried up the hall, jammed his feet into a pair of sneakers, and pulled the front door closed behind him. He held his backpack over his head as an umbrella and ran up the path. The back door of the car hung open, and Olive was inside. Mum slammed the front passenger door shut and fastened her seat belt.

"See you in seven minutes," Dad said into his phone. He threw it into Mum's lap. "Turn that off for me. Get in, Ben!" he said, revving the engine.

Ben slid into the backseat. "The police just came to our house!" he said, breathless. He heaved the door closed as Dad spun the car around, laying rubber on the road. "What are you doing? Where are we going?"

No one said anything.

"Mum?"

"Vacation," Mum said.

They had never been on a vacation before. Ben got up on his knees and looked through the dirty back window. Golden was still tied to the rusted, doorless car on the front lawn.

"What about G—"

"Nan's coming to get her," Mum said. "Put your seat belt on."

Ben heard a siren as the car swung around the corner onto the old highway.

"Red light!" Mum shouted.

Dad kept driving.

No one said anything for a few minutes. Olive sat there, looking out the window, sucking her thumb and clutching Bonzo, her dirty, gray stuffed rabbit.

Car yards flicked by.

"Where are we going on vacation?" Ben asked.

Dad adjusted his side and rearview mirrors, weaving between cars, vans, and semitrailers.

"Mum?"

She did not respond. Everything felt odd. Maybe it was because Ben had never been on a vacation before. Maybe because the police had just knocked on their door. He slumped down on the backseat, thinking.

"Why are we in such a damn hurry?" he asked.

"Watch your language!" Mum said.

"Did you hear me say that the *police* just came to our house?" Ben continued. "And why didn't you tell me this morning that we were going away?"

Dad hit himself on the forehead four times with a fist. "That kid asks too many questions!"

"Sorry," Ben said.

"Don't apologize all the time," Dad snapped. "It's weak."

"Sorry," he said again.

"The vacation was a surprise," Mum told him. "You're always asking about a trip. This is it. Our first family vacation."

It felt weird to hear Mum saying "family vacation." They weren't really one of those family-movie-night, camp-in-the-backyard, let's-discuss-this-and-get-everyone's-opinion kind of families. They were more of a dinner-in-front-of-the-TV, key's-under-the-mat, if-you-want-breakfast-make-it-yourself kind of family.

"Can I bring a friend?" Ben asked.

"No," his parents both said at once.

"But James took Gus when he went on vacation."

No one said anything.

"Where are we going?"

Rain drummed on the car roof as they charged past a gas station, a funeral home, a fried chicken place.

"Just up the coast," Mum said, looking at Dad, who looked from road to rearview mirror and back again.

"Where to? Gosford?"

"No."

"Kings Bay? We're going to the beach in Kings Bay!" Ben said excitedly. He had wanted to go to Kings Bay ever since Nan sent him a postcard from there when he was little.

"No."

Mum's phone pinged. She picked it up and started typing.

"Turn it off!" Dad said.

"Why?"

Dad gave her a fierce look.

Mum switched off the phone.

Ben and Olive glanced sideways at one another. They had never seen their mother switch her phone off before.

Mum turned and looked through the gap between headrest and seat. "We're going to the cabin."

"Yessss!" Olive said, raising both arms in the air, then plugging her thumb back into her mouth.

"Boooooo!" Ben said. "I don't want to. I want to go home. I'm in the middle of making my movie."

He had been hearing about his grandfather's cabin in the hills behind Kings Bay all his life. When Dad was a kid Pop went up there, fishing and hunting rabbits, a couple of times a year. Dad said he was hardly ever allowed to go, even though he'd really wanted to. Ben knew Dad had taken Mum there once before Ben was born.

Nature wasn't Ben's favorite thing—freaky insects, animals, dirt. He preferred being in his room playing games, watching TV, eating. This had never been a problem because the Silvers had not left the suburbs in the twelve years since Ben was born.

"Get out of the way!" Dad yelled at someone.

Dad was skinny and serious. An ex-mechanic, salesman, now car wrecker. He wore an armful of tattoos, black wraparound sunglasses, and a dirty cap with a gas company logo on it. In the rearview mirror, Ben could see Dad's chipped front tooth. He looked ratlike.

Ben sometimes wondered how Dad had ended up with Mum. April Silver: ten years younger than Dad, tall, brown hair. People said she could have been a model years ago, but then Ben was born and that changed everything. So now she worked at the wreckers instead. Dad thought he ran the business, but Mum did. Ben knew.

Ben sat back and looked out the window at the signs going by. AAA Lighting. Craig's Concreting. The Golden Wok. He thought about the police and squeezed his bottom lip. He closed his eyes and saw his stop-motion movie playing on the movie screen at the back of his eyelids. He saw what he had already shot—the crime, the car chase, then the run through the forest. Maybe heading toward a creepy cabin. It wasn't in the script yet but maybe they would find a cabin, the zombie thief's hideout—abandoned, trees hanging low over the roof.

The car jerked and revved hard as Dad flung it back a gear. Ben's eyes snapped open, ending his imaginary movie.

They hurried along the old highway, wipers scraping the windshield. Ben didn't mind his characters going to a creepy cabin but he did not want to go to one himself. He wanted to be back in his room, happy, comfortable. He tried to think of anything that might stall them.

"What about clothes and stuff? I'm still in my school uniform."

"It's all right," Mum said. "We'll get new ones."

"New clothes?"

"Yep. That's what you do on a vacation."

Ben thought about this for a second. He had never heard of it before.

"I thought you guys hated vacations," he said.

Dad laughed, which Ben liked. Usually Dad only laughed when he was with his friends at a football game.

"What about school?" Ben said. "We just had a school holiday."

"Now you've got another," Mum said.

"Can you please tell Maugrim to slow down," Olive said quietly, then stuck her thumb back into her mouth.

"You tell him," Ben said.

Olive shook her head. She had not spoken to Dad in over a week. One night at dinner, during a TV commercial, she had called him Maugrim, the evil wolf from *The Lion, the Witch and the Wardrobe*. Dad was so angry when he found out who Maugrim was, he sent her to her room with no dessert and put Bonzo away for a week. Since then she had only spoken to Dad when necessary and only through an interpreter. Olive did that kind of thing sometimes. She was a tough little kid. Ben would never dare stand up to Dad like that.

Dad checked his rearview and side mirrors and took a sharp right in front of oncoming traffic. Ben was thrown sideways toward Olive, who shoved him away. "Get off me. You stink like poo," she said.

Ben sat up. Dad swung a fast left, then gunned it up a street lined with brown brick houses. They were a bit nicer than Ben's house. Most had basketball hoops and toys and bikes strewn around the yard. Two kids in yellow raincoats ran off the road as Dad powered toward them. Half a block farther up, he pulled into a driveway where a man stood next to an empty garage. He wore a white, pin-striped business shirt and black pants. He was tall and skinny with ginger-colored hair, thinning on top. Uncle Chris. Even though he lived so close, they had not seen Dad's brother in over a year. Dad drove into the garage, switched off the engine, and got out.

"Does Dad still think Uncle Chris is an idiot?" Olive asked.

"Shhh," Mum said. "He's arranged for a new car for us to drive on our trip." She gathered her things.

"What?" Ben asked.

Mum ignored him. "Everyone out."

Ben looked through the back window to where Dad was shaking his brother's hand. Uncle Chris gave Dad a gray nylon sports bag with black handles and looked over at Ben. Then they walked up the driveway to an old station wagon parked in the street.

VACATION HAIRCUTS

Clumps of hair fell to the ugly orange tiles of the motel bathroom.

"Hold still," Mum said.

"How much are you cutting off?" Ben asked. "I don't wanna have a haircut."

"Don't be silly. We're all having haircuts."

"Why?"

"Vacation haircuts," she said. "That's what you do on a vacation."

"As if," Ben said. The only guy he could remember coming back from a vacation with a haircut was Robert Dewar, who lived two doors up from Nan. He'd fallen asleep chewing gum and it went all through his hair and he had to have it shaved. He'd returned to school bald.

"It's looking better already," Mum said. "I forgot you had eyes."

"Have you ever cut hair before?" Ben asked, doubtful.

"You know I've always wanted to. I'm going to cut mine in a minute," she said, snipping carefully away at his bangs. Ben could see her fingernails close up, bitten back to the nail bed. The tips of her fingers looked red and sore.

"I hope you do as bad a job on yours as you're doing on mine," Ben said. "And why aren't you cutting Olive's?"

"Her hair's too beautiful. She can wear pigtails or a bun. Look down," Mum said, her tongue poking out as she concentrated on clipping around Ben's ear.

"Why don't we just wait till morning and go to a hairdresser?" Ben asked.

They had been driving for about five hours when the rain became too heavy to see the road. The wipers on the car Uncle Chris had given them did not work well. Ben couldn't work out why they had bothered swapping—the car was even older than the Green Machine. They had pulled off the highway into Rest Haven, a deadbeat motel with a flickering fluorescent sign out front.

"Don't use your whiny voice," Mum said.

She often accused him of whining, so Ben said in his deepest, most manly voice, "Why don't we just go to a hairdresser?"

"It's more fun this way," she said.

"What's fun about having your hair hacked off by a maniac with a pair of nail scissors?"

"Mind your tongue," she said. "Head down."

Ben watched another handful of thick brown hair drop to the tiles. There was more hair on the floor than Ben remembered having on his head. Another large clump fell. He looked up into the mirror again, and a tiny scream leaped from his mouth. His hair was an inch long.

"I think it looks good," Mum said. "More like a boy."

"Good? I look like a toilet brush!"

"Oh, stop complaining, you big boob," she said.

"Boob?" he said, raising his voice and standing up. "I'm not a 'boob.' People are going to be cleaning toilets with my head."

"Sit!" Mum said, like she was speaking to Golden.

"No," Ben said.

"Oi!" he heard from the next room.

He looked at Mum, thinking for a second. There was no point getting Dad upset. He turned and studied his reflection in the mirror. "This room is where hair comes to die."

"It's a new look."

"Vacation haircuts," he grunted as he flopped back into the chair.

A grin spread over Mum's lips as she tidied up the sides.

"I'm hungry," Ben said.

"Well, we don't have anything. It won't hurt you to skip a few meals."

Ben looked at her in the mirror. She knew he was paranoid about his weight because he'd told her the things kids said at school. She gave him an apologetic look and kept cutting.

"Ow!" he said, grabbing his ear. He looked at his hand. Blood.

"I'm sorry, I'm sorry, I'm sorry. Let me look at it."

Ben stormed out of the bathroom, squeezing his ear to stop the blood flow. The room was dimly lit with brick walls, a double bed, and a tired-looking couch. Dad was looking out the window through a gap in the faded pink curtains, speaking to someone on the motel phone. Olive was asleep on the bed with Bonzo, lit by the glow of a greyhound race on TV.

"Ben!" Mum called.

He headed for the front door and yanked it open but the security chain stopped it.

"Hey!" Dad said, putting the phone down.

"What?"

"Has your mother finished with you?"

Ben reached for his ear. He dabbed at it and showed Dad the blood seeping into the shallow channels of his fingerprints. If he was honest there wasn't actually much blood. He would have liked there to be a bit more, but it was still blood. Mum came out of the bathroom.

"Yes," he said. "She's finished."

Dad looked at Mum. Mum looked at Ben. Ben looked at Dad. And that is how his hair stayed. Short and spiky with sticky-uppy bits.

Dad was in the butcher's chair next. He swore a lot and Mum threatened to cut his ear off too if he didn't stop complaining. He stopped.

Ben sat on a green vinyl chair that had a dodgy leg, opened the curtains a little wider, and stared into the parking lot through the rain-drizzled window. He grabbed his brown leather notebook from his bag. Ben had found the notebook in the cramped office at the back of Nan's house where she kept candy bars in the middle drawer of a rolltop desk. The notebook had been his grandfather's. When Pop was alive he had jotted some numbers on the front pages. Sums written in smudgy blue ink. Ben could barely read the writing but he kept those pages in the book.

At the back of the notebook, on the last page, there was another bit of Pop's scrawly writing. These words: "An old man tells his grandson one evening that there is a battle raging inside him, inside all of us. A terrible battle between two wolves. One wolf is bad—pride, envy, jealousy, greed. The other wolf is good—kindness, hope, love, truth. The child asks, 'Which wolf will win?' The grandfather answers simply, 'The one you feed.'"

Ben liked the words. He liked that they were from Pop, who had died when Ben was two. Nan said that, up until then, the two of them had been inseparable. Pop had taken him everywhere, always repeating a rhyme that Ben had loved: "Ben Silver is no good. Chop him up for firewood. If he is no good for that, feed him to the old tomcat."

Ben chewed on the rubber end of his pencil for a moment before writing this list:

Police
Vacation
Uncle Chris. Gray nylon bag. Black handles.
The new old car
Haircuts

Vacations were rubbish, Ben decided. And the cabin would be even worse. Nature. Ben wondered how long it would be till they could go home and he could finish making his movie. He was going to miss ordering his lunch at school tomorrow. And soccer at lunchtime. Why couldn't James or Gus have come on vacation with them?

Cars pulled in and out of the parking lot, headlights shining on hundreds of little raindrop jewels racing down the window. Out front, the sign for Rest Haven flickered to an uneven beat. The cranky lady from reception crossed the parking lot holding a red umbrella, a small carton of milk, and some towels. She looked at Ben, quickly looked away, but then glanced back. He wondered if she thought his hair was odd. Or just his family.

When they checked in, Dad had refused to show her his driver's license, saying that he'd lost his wallet. Ben had seen him with his wallet at a gas station on the highway half an hour earlier, so he went out to the car, brought Dad's wallet to him, and said, "Here it is!" But, rather than being thankful, Dad was angry.

"Don't stick your big bib in!" he shouted as they drove across to the parking space in front of their room.

Ben didn't even wear a bib. What did "stick your big bib in" mean?

Soon Dad emerged from the bathroom with close-cropped hair—another unhappy customer. Ben tried not to laugh.

"Go to sleep," Dad grunted, switching off the TV and lamp and flopping onto the big bed.

Ben lay down on the couch in a rectangle of light from the bathroom. When Mum appeared half an hour later she was hardly recognizable. Her hair, usually halfway down her back, was now boyish and weird-looking.

"Why did you do that?" Ben asked.

"Go to sleep. We leave early."

He watched her. She laid Olive down on a blanket on the floor and sat on the edge of the bed with her back to him for a long while.

"How early do we leave?" Ben whispered into the darkness.

"Four."

"Why?"

"Because your father says so . . . Go to sleep."

Ben lay there, eyes open, listening to rain beating the roof. The couch cushions smelled moldy and felt itchy. He wondered if there were bedbugs. He imagined his body swarming with mini beasts, hundreds of thousands of them eating him alive. He closed his eyes and saw it like a stop-motion movie with tiny bedbugs made of clay.

Dad's snoring filled the room.

Ben tried not to think about the bites. He thought about Nan, his dad's mum. She lived around the corner from them, right on the highway. She always had time for him and was interested in what he had to say. Nan was rake-thin, a tough old bird, one of those old people who sat on the front steps watching the world go by. Ben wondered if she had picked up Golden. Even though it was past midnight, he knew that Nan would be lying awake in bed, staring at the ceiling, listening to talk radio and world news. She only slept for a couple of hours just before dawn.

Ben's eyes closed. He thought about the four police officers. He had asked Mum about them again, and she muttered something unconvincing about old parking tickets.

Ben touched his spiky hair and scratched his skin. He felt hungry. He silently prayed for the vacation to be over soon.

CHASE

Adrenaline streaked through him. He craned his neck to look out the back window.

Mum looked too.

"Don't!" Dad snapped.

"What does he want?" Ben asked. "Is he after us? Were we speeding?"

Dad drove on. He hadn't taken a break in five hours.

Olive knelt and stared out the back window, sucking her thumb.

"Sit," Ben whispered, but she didn't listen. This was not a surprise.

"Are you going to pull over?" Mum asked.

They rode on in silence. Ben wondered if Dad had heard her.

There were two short, sharp blasts on the siren.

Ben had never wanted anything more than to look out the back window. Adults were strange. If kids ran the world everybody would be allowed to look when the police were following them. Not just annoying little sisters.

"What are you doing?" Mum asked. "Shouldn't you pull over?"

Dad shrugged. "We haven't done anything."

"Ray, it's the *police*."

Dad wiped his nose on the back of his hand and kept driving. "I haven't done anything."

They drove on.

"If we haven't done anything, won't they let us go?" Ben said helpfully. Surely that made sense to his father. When Ben became a police officer, if he pulled someone over and they hadn't done anything, he would let them go, for sure.

An engine roared and a car moved up quickly beside them. The vehicle was royal blue with a white-and-blue checker print, dark-tinted windows, and four antennas. Ben knew what all of the antennas were for. He had sat in a police car at the Royal Easter Show a few years ago and committed every detail to memory. One was an 800 MHz enhancer. Another was a VHF low band antenna. Another for 468 MHz and then the standard radio antenna above the back window.

The lights and siren weren't on but the police officer—black wraparound sunglasses, short spiky hair, square head—pointed directly at Dad, then to the side of the road.

Olive started to giggle. "He looks *an*gry," she said. Olive wanted to be a robber when she grew up. And a judge.

Dad swore under his breath but Ben heard it.

Mum chewed what was left of her nails.

Ben watched the cop.

Dad kept driving.

Tension spilled from the gaps around the windows and dripped down the sides of the car. With a low growl, Dad pulled onto the crunchy gravel shoulder of the road. He kept the engine running. They waited.

Ben caught a glimpse of movement in the side mirror as the officer stepped out of his car, put on his police cap, shut his door, and walked along the edge of the road toward them. He had a wide, steady walk, his legs far apart, his body like a gum tree trunk. He wore a light blue shirt, dark blue pants, dusty black boots. His pistol was slung low, strapped to his thigh with a harness.

He stopped beside the car. His left arm was heavily tattooed, like Dad's. Ben was surprised that police were allowed to have tattoos.

Dad rolled down the window. Mum smiled at the policeman.

"Can you please turn your engine off?"

Dad twisted the key and the car became still and quiet. Just the *click* and *tick* of the hot motor. And the *tock-tock-tock-tock* of the blinker.

"Why didn't you slow down?" the officer asked.

"I didn't see you at first."

"Did you hear my siren?"

Dad sat for a few seconds, then nodded.

"Well, why didn't you pull over?"

Dad waited. "I'm not sure."

"Make sure you pull over more quickly in the future."

Dad nodded.

Ben was listening so intently he forgot to breathe. He stared out the window at the officer, whose thick reddish neck seemed to burst from his collar into a roll of fat that ended at his tight-fitting police cap. He looked about ten years younger than Dad. Early thirties. His name badge read "Dan Toohey." A good name for a police officer. Not as good as Ben Silver, but good.

"Is this your car?" the officer asked.

"Yes," Dad said.

Ben bit his tongue.

"Do you know why I'm pulling you over?"

Dad sat there. Mum chewed on her finger. Ben still could not get used to her short, weed-whacker haircut.

Dad shook his head. "No."

"You have no idea?"

Dad shook his head again.

Dan Toohey looked in at Olive and Ben sitting there in their school uniforms. A semitrailer thundered by, ruffling the officer's shirt. Ben leaned forward in his seat, his right ear twisted toward the action so he would not miss anything.

"Your blinker," the officer said. "You've had your blinker on for about five miles, you dodo." He smiled for the first time, then he laughed, a big policeman's belly laugh.

Dad looked down and turned off his blinker. He laughed too. It was a bit forced. Then Mum laughed and Ben tried to laugh, even though he didn't think it was that funny.

"That was all. But since you didn't want to pull over, I'll have to run your license, all right?" The laughter petered out. "It'll only take two seconds."

Dad took his time finding his wallet. Ben could see it on the dashboard but he didn't say anything.

"It's on the dash," Dan Toohey said.

"Oh." Dad passed his license through the window.

"Ray Silver . . . Back in a minute."

"Excuse me," Ben said to the officer from the backseat.

Mum shot him a glare.

"Do you have any police things you give to kids?" Ben felt like an idiot so he added, "For my sister."

"Is not, Poo Face!" Olive said. "It's for him!"

"No, yeah, no worries. Let me think. I'll have a look in the car for you."

"It's okay," Dad said. "Don't worry about it. He's just—"

"No trouble at all. It's good to encourage the young ones. Otherwise the fire department gets all the new recruits. You a budding officer?" He smiled at Ben, who felt embarrassed and didn't say anything. "Actually, you know what I've got? They've just started giving us these business cards and I dunno what to do with them." Dan Toohey took a velcro wallet from his back pocket and passed a card through to Ben.

It bore the name Dan Toohey and his rank, constable, with the New South Wales police logo—a circle of green leaves with a red crown on top and a wedge-tailed eagle in the center. At the bottom were the words *Culpam Poena Premit Comes.*

"Maybe you can use it like a policeman's badge or something," Dan Toohey said.

Ben looked up and said quietly, "Thanks."

"I'll just run this license. Back in a minute."

Dan Toohey headed to his car.

"What'd you ask that for?" Dad said.

"I—"

"He's just excited," Mum cut in.

"Baby," Dad said under his breath, shaking his head.

They sat in silence, the car filling with tension once more now that Dan Toohey and his belly laugh were gone. Trucks roared by, rocking the car with wind-rush.

Ben studied the business card, mouthing the words "*Culpam Poena Premit Comes*" over and over again. He flicked open his notebook, slipped the card in, and wrote the words on the inside cover, pressing hard to etch into the leather.

Culpam Poena Premit Comes

"Hey, Mum, what does '*Culpam Poena Premit Comes*' mean?" He stumbled over the words.

"I don't know. I don't speak Chinese," she said.

Mum seemed to call any language she didn't understand "Chinese."

"Dad?"

He was looking in the side mirror on his door. "Neither do I."

"You guys are old. Didn't you do Latin at school?"

Ben was thrust back into his seat as Dad floored the accelerator, spinning the wheels, spitting gravel.

They drove away. Fast.

Ben looked at the reflection of Dad's eyes in the rearview mirror. Mum looked back at the police car sitting beside the road. Olive opened her mouth and stared at Dad, thumb frozen in midair a few inches from her face.

"Wasn't he coming back?" Ben asked. "You left your license."

Dad drove on, sitting up, arms straight, holding the wheel firmly with two hands now. He took the next exit up the road. Ben heard the siren as they turned right at the bottom of the exit ramp. They sped underneath an overpass and along a winding, narrow road past fields of sugar cane. The siren sound was moving closer when Dad took a sharp left down a dirt track. It was a trail between two fields of tall green cane. Ben sat up and looked back as their car fishtailed.

Dad turned right down another dirt track and slammed on the brakes, switching the engine off.

Sheets of dust blew in through the open windows. Ben heard the police car dart by on the road. His heart pummeled his chest.

Olive laughed. "That was fun."

They sat, engine off, sound of a crow *caw*ing in the sugar cane nearby, siren in the distance, dirt settling all around them. For the first time ever, Ben did not ask a question. Mum sniffed and covered her mouth and nose with one hand.

They sat.

"Must've been after someone else," Dad said.

The siren faded.

"You got any of that drink left?" Dad asked.

Ben picked up the soft drink bottle from the seat next to him and handed it to Dad, who guzzled it all and wiped the corners of his mouth with the back of his hand.

"What do we do now, Ray?" Mum asked.

"Stay here for a bit," Dad said. "Then keep going up to the cabin."

WITHIN THE WOODS

Ben awoke to darkness all around as the car climbed a steep hill into rain-foresty woods. Trees flicked quickly by. Tiny red eyes watched them from the blackness. Mum and Olive were asleep, Dad lit by dashboard glow.

Ben stretched and groaned. "Where are we?"

No answer.

The car raced ever upward.

Ben's back and muscles ached. His neck hurt. They had been driving all day, and he had fallen asleep after a drive-thru dinner of burger and fries.

"Dad?" he asked again.

"Nearly there."

"The cabin?"

Silence.

Ben sat, quiet and wide awake. The headlights sliced through the night, opening it up for a moment, then snapping it shut as they passed. He nervously touched each one of his fingertips to his thumbs over and over again. He had seven million questions surging through him but he did not know how to ask Dad without riling him.

I'm me, he thought. *Not this again,* said another voice inside him. *But if I'm me, then who is everybody else?* Ben often had these "I'm me" sessions. It was usually when he was walking home from school or before he went to sleep. *What does that mean—"me"?* he wondered. He sometimes drove himself crazy with these thoughts. He tried to concentrate on the road, the headlight beams, the flattened animal carcasses. Cane toads sitting up, tall and proud, then *bam.* Tires. Pancake.

Thoughts drifted out of the darkness. *I am me. But if I'm me, then who are Mum and Dad? Who are James and Gus? Are they "me" too? They think they're "me." They call themselves "I" just like I do. So how am I different? I'm in a different body but are we the same thing somehow?*

Ben's "I'm me" sessions always brought up more questions than answers. Each time he tried to capture "me," it would disappear into the dark corners of his mind, like a dream he was desperately trying to remember. Where did his thoughts and ideas come from? Even the thought "I'm me"—what was that? It felt like there was someone back there saying things that Ben couldn't control. His mind flicked between sharp corners, darting animals, dashboard glow, and "me" until Dad suddenly slowed on a corner and took a left onto a dirt road.

"Is this it?" Ben asked.

Dad skidded to a stop. He nudged Mum.

"I think this is it."

Mum stirred and sat up in her seat. Her jaw clicked when she yawned—a childhood collision with a wire fence. "What?"

"I'm not sure but I think this is it."

Mum looked around. Trees. Dirt road. Dark. "Okay."

"I went through that little town with the water tank and the store with the metal cow out front, then uphill for about ten minutes and . . ."

Mum thought for a moment. "I don't know. I just woke up. I haven't been here in years. Maybe it is."

Silence all around. Headlights trained on tree trunks. Eucalypts. Olive out cold. Ben waiting, nervous.

"Well, should we go down and check?" Dad asked.

"It's your family's cabin."

"What do you mean by that?"

"I mean that you've dragged us up here, so you make the decision," Mum said.

Dad waited a few seconds, then the car began to climb steeply downhill. Olive's head was tossed around by every bump in the road. Trees crowded in overhead. Ben was alert and focused on the steep track diving into the valley. Questions about "me" were left back on the paved road. He wished that they were arriving in the day. Dad drove slowly, weaving to avoid potholes. Something shot out from the side of the road and bounced in front of the car. Dad hit the brakes.

"What was that?" Ben asked, squeezing his lip.

"Dunno," Dad said. "Wasn't a rabbit. Nose was too long."

"A bandicoot, maybe? Or a potoroo?"

"What's that?" Dad asked.

"Don't worry." Ben wasn't too sure himself but there was no point talking Australian wildlife with his old man. It wasn't Dad's thing.

They plunged ever downward, the ridges and ruts in the road becoming deeper the farther they drove. For five minutes nobody spoke.

Ben figured that every future vacation could only be better than this. He clutched the broken armrest in his door and dug his feet into the floor. The nose of the car was pitched so far forward it felt as though they might somersault.

Bang! The front right wheel dropped. They stopped.

Dad set the handbrake, opened his door, and climbed out to inspect the damage. Hum of engine, chill of night, and smell of fumes filled the car. The lights were trained on a sharp left-hand bend farther down the road. It looked like a steep drop over the edge of the bend.

"Do you think this is the right way?" Ben whispered, careful Dad did not hear.

Mum shrugged, chewing on the skin of her thumb.

A minute or two passed before Dad got back into the car. "Can't see a thing."

He released the handbrake and turned the wheel far to the left, his door still open. He revved hard, and the back wheels spun, howling into the night. Ben prayed that they would get out of this, but the car didn't move. Mum sighed. Ben balled his fists, digging his nails into his palms. He wondered how Olive could sleep.

The engine screamed, and the wheels continued to spin. Dad turned the wheel to the right, and the front of the car jerked suddenly up and forward. Dad slammed his door, and they lurched ahead, toward the sharp left-hand bend.

Dad took the corner too fast, and the back of the car slipped toward the drop, then corrected. Soon, bushes bunched in on either side of them. *Screeeeek.* Branches scratching. Dad growled. The *screeeeek* went on, digging its claws into the paintwork, before a clearing appeared ahead and the bushes opened up on either side.

"This is it," Dad said.

A timber cabin came into view, hunched against the forest and darkness. It was built of long logs, half a foot thick, running straight up and down from ground to roof. One dark window and a door next to it. Trees huddled low over the cabin just as Ben had imagined, the ridges in the corrugated iron roof choked with leaves.

The car came to a stop. Dad twisted the key and switched off the engine.

"I'm not getting out," Ben said.

THE DEAD OF NIGHT

"Yes, you are," Dad said.

Cabin. Dark, sad, villainous.

"Are you really sure this is it?" Ben asked.

"Yes. I'm sure," Dad replied, a trickle of venom in his voice.

"We'll stay in the car," Mum said.

Ben was quiet.

Dad looked at him. "Big girl," he said under his breath. "Y'scared?"

Dad knew that Ben didn't like being called a "girl" or "scared."

Dad opened his door.

Ben opened his. The *shhhhhh* of water rushed into the car, a river or stream nearby. Ben stepped out, quietly clicked his door closed, and moved toward the cabin, half a step behind his father. He scanned the ground for snakes, every cell in his body pleading to return to the car. A frog croaked loudly nearby. Insects sang a never-ending song in the trees all around. The headlights cast monstrous moving shadows of Ben and Dad onto the cabin. Ben felt a bite on his arm and slapped it. There was a call from deep within the woods to the right that sounded like a baby's cry.

"What's that?" Ben grabbed Dad's tattooed arm and fell into step beside him.

"Night birds," Dad said quietly. "I s'pose."

They arrived at the door. Ben looked back at the car. Mum was hidden behind the starry headlight flare.

Dad tried the door handle. It didn't open. There was a rusted metal keyhole. Dad swore and went to the window, trying to get the tips of his fingers into the cracks and lift.

"Don't we have a key?" Ben asked.

Dad did not respond. After a minute or two he banged his fist on the timber window frame and looked back to the car, squinting, his face bright white.

"Can't we get in?" Mum called, her door open the slightest crack.

"I'm thinking," Dad said quietly, then he disappeared around the side of the cabin.

"Dad?"

For a moment Ben could hear his father's footsteps snapping twigs and leaves and then there was nothing. Ben went to the corner of the cabin and looked down the side. The ground sloped steeply toward the sound of rushing water. The back of the cabin looked like it was up on stilts.

"Dad?" he called into the darkness. Something moved on the cabin wall near his face. A spider, hairy, running up one of the logs. He jerked away, a strangled *gargh* escaping his throat.

"Dad?" Ben called, louder this time.

Nothing.

Ben took a few tentative steps down the side of the building. The ground fell away quickly, and he slipped, falling on his backside. He jumped to his feet and climbed back up to the corner of the cabin.

"Boo!" Dad said. Ben screamed. Dad laughed. He had circled the cabin and returned to the front door.

"I'm gonna have to kick it in," Dad said. He looked at the door like he was about to fight it, then rammed his shoulder into it, but it didn't budge.

He turned sideways, took two steps back. He lifted his right leg and gave the door an almighty kick, right next to the handle. There was a fierce wood-splitting crack and the door exploded open. Dad fell inside, coming down on his knees. The bush fell silent. Something scurried across the cabin roof.

"We bring a flashlight?" he called to Mum, shielding his eyes from the headlights.

"No," came the reply.

"I asked you to get a flashlight at that gas station," he said.

"No, you didn't."

"Well, I thought about it," he said to himself.

Ben stood at the door and looked into the cabin. The headlights cut through the cracks between tall upright logs, lighting the room in long, thin slits.

"Comin' in?" Dad asked.

Ben could taste acid in the back of his throat. The cabin had a sickening stench of mold and dead things. He pulled the neck of his school shirt up over his nose. He wanted to be back in his bedroom with the comforting smell of his own dirty clothes and discarded cereal bowls. But Ben knew that when he was a police officer he might be called to places like this every night of the week. He needed to practice. He needed to "man up," like Dad always said. He took a step forward. The cabin was a single room about twenty feet wide and fifteen feet deep. Something scuttled into a large, open cupboard at the back.

"We're not sleeping in here, are we?" Ben asked, furiously kneading his sweaty hands.

"Where else are we going to sleep?" Dad said, turning to Ben with a smile, a thin beam of light slicing his face in two.

Ben began to wonder if he really had what it took to be a cop. Could he do this kind of thing for a living? Maybe he was destined to be a paper pusher back at the station, eating doughnuts, drinking coffee. (Ben thought dreamily about the half-finished jam doughnut on the plate in his bedroom.) Or maybe he could ditch the whole becoming-a-detective idea and make stop-motion movies or design games or work for Lego instead. Ben stopped wringing his hands.

"Are you two okay?" Mum called.

They looked at one another through the gloom, Dad inside the cabin, Ben in the doorway. He squeezed his lip so hard that he almost drew blood.

"Sorry. I'm sleeping in the car," Ben said. He turned, walked away, and ripped open the car door.

"Big baby!" Dad called.

Ben threw himself into the backseat and pulled the door shut behind him. It was warm and happy in there, and it smelled caramelly, like Olive when she slept. He was never going into that cabin again.

"Is it okay?" Mum asked.

"Beautiful," Ben said. "You'll love it."

THE BAG

Ben stood outside the closed cabin door, still wearing his school shirt and shorts from two days ago. Olive stood beside him, hair mussed up, holding Bonzo the rabbit by one long, grubby ear. She wore her uniform too, a light green summer dress. Feet bare, as always. No shoe had been invented that was comfortable enough for Olive.

Early morning light poked at the cabin through sky-high pine trees. Mum was passed out in the car, still parked in the sandy clearing in front of the small timber building.

Ben's heart went *blump, blump, blump.* He could hear his father inside. A piece of furniture scraped across the floor. He waited a few seconds before giving the door a little push. It swung open with a *raaaaaaark.*

Dad stood on a chair in the dim light of the room, reaching up into the open roof area. Exposed timber beams ran from one side of the room to the other. No ceiling. Just the rusty corrugated iron of the peaked roof high above. Dad looked down at Ben and Olive.

"Get out of here!" He quickly covered something with a piece of black plastic. "What are you doing sneaking around?"

He jumped off the chair and stormed toward them. Ben and Olive backed away. He slammed the door in their faces.

Mum sat up, woken by the sound, and opened her car door. "What?"

Olive giggled.

"What are you laughing at?" Ben whispered.

"Dad being cranky. What was he doing?"

"Are you guys all right?" Mum asked.

"Yes, but Dad has poo in his pants. Again," Olive said.

That almost made Ben smile, but his pounding heart stifled the grin before it reached his lips.

"What's for breakfast?" Olive asked. "I want sugar on toast. Can we have sugar on toast?"

"We don't have anything. There's half a Kit Kat but you can't have that for breakfast. We'll work something out," Mum said, closing her door and lying back in her seat.

"Can you hear water? Maybe it's a river," Olive said. "Let's go exploring."

"I want to go home," Ben said. He headed to the car as the cabin door opened.

"We've got to clean this place out so we can sleep in it tonight," Dad said.

"I want to go home."

"Well, you're not. You're helping me clean up. You think I want to do it? No, but some things in life just have to be done."

Ben looked into his father's eyes, deciding whether or not to challenge him. Dad was still a good foot taller than him—thin but strong, lean arm muscles tanned dark.

Some vacation, Ben thought, but he dared not say it.

Dad went back inside. Ben followed and was smacked with the stench of mold and death. He looked around. There was a shelf on the back wall, jammed with things. Next to it, a creepy walk-in cupboard with large doors yawning open. On the right-hand wall, a solid timber workbench and a small, rusty green trunk. Under a window, a wooden dining table and chair. To the left, behind the front door, there was a torn camp bed with a grubby sheet and leaves on the floor all around it. Up high, another window that had been smashed. And the clump of black plastic sitting on a wide timber slat up in the roof beams.

"Get to work. We'll chuck most of it out," Dad grunted. "And don't ever sneak up on me like that again, y'hear?"

Ben nodded.

"What?" Dad snapped.

"Yes, Dad," Ben said.

He scanned the floor for rats, spiders, snakes.

Over the next three hours, as the sun climbed high in the sky, they pulled everything out of the cabin and laid it on the ground in the clearing. Ben was forced to sweep, de-web, and throw stacks of old, moldy junk down the side of the cabin. Dad wanted to get rid of most of Pop's things.

Ben saw seventeen spiders. Every time he screamed or jumped back Dad would help him get over it by saying something like "You want me to put a nappy on you? Just hit it with your shoe."

Olive didn't do anything. She just poked her tongue out and asked the same knock-knock joke over and over again. "Knock knock. Who's there? Banana. Banana who? Banana walking down the street with his head split open." She made it up herself. Ben didn't think she understood the principles of knock-knock jokes and he threatened to split her head open if she told him the joke again. Which she did. But he did not.

Ben stole a look at the black plastic in the open roof space. He tried to imagine what it might be. What would his father hide in the roof and get so angry about? Chocolate? Beer?

As he worked, Ben found interesting things—peacock feathers, a heavy chain with a brass padlock, handmade arrows, two metal traps with tough steel jaws, and an old, open safe with a combination lock. Dad sat and looked at it for a long time. When Ben asked Dad why he was looking at it, Dad snorted and muttered something about Pop, then chucked the safe down the side of the cabin.

Ben found a copy of a book called *My Side of the Mountain*. He wasn't a big reader, but the book had an interesting cover—a kid in the wilderness with an eagle or a falcon flying down to sit on his arm. Ben suspected that things could get boring out here, so he slipped the thin book into the back pocket of his school shorts.

He asked Dad about things that he found, trying to make conversation as they worked, but Dad was even more distracted than usual. Ben desperately wanted to ask him what was going on with the cops and coming to the cabin and the thing in the roof and why Dad was so angry and when they could go home, but he thought better of it.

In the large, dark cupboard at the back, Ben found a hunting gun, old and rusty, and a bow for the arrows. He asked Dad about the gun and bow, and Dad grunted something about Pop hunting rabbits and left the room.

Fishing rods, a shovel, loose pieces of timber. And that clump of black plastic. Ben wanted to ignore it but would-be detectives are curious by nature.

Mum was speaking to Dad out near the car. Ben tiptoed across the cabin and listened carefully from just inside the door.

"Tell me when we're leaving," Mum said in a low voice. "We're in the middle of nowhere."

"I think that's the idea."

"There's no running water, no toilet. There's not even *phone* reception. I *hate* it."

"Read your magazine," Dad snipped.

"This wasn't the deal."

"Let's just pretend we're adults for a minute, April. Think about it," Dad said. "Oi, Big Ears!"

Ben knew who Dad was talking about. He poked his head into the doorway. Dad gave Mum a look and walked toward Ben, who swallowed hard. Dad placed a hand on the back of his neck and spun him around so that they were both looking into the cabin.

"What do you think?" Dad said. The room was cleaned, restored, and only smelled vaguely of mold now.

"Not bad," Ben said.

"Apart from listening in on conversations, you've played hard, done good." Dad took his hand off Ben's neck. "Pull my finger."

Ben did.

Parp. A sharp, loud trumpet sound from Dad's behind.

"Ray!" Mum said.

Ben laughed, but Dad didn't crack a smile. He never did, which made it even funnier.

"I've got to find some reception up the hill, make some calls." Dad headed for the car, grabbing his new phone off the front seat. He had bought himself and Mum new phones on the way up the coast and dumped their old ones in a garbage can outside the store. He walked off up the dirt road.

Ben watched until he disappeared around the corner. Mum went back to the far side of the clearing to lie on a rock in the sun. Olive sang loudly to herself and marched up and down a low tree branch, holding the branch above her for stability, barking orders to invisible people on the ground, something about her kingdom and loyal subjects. Ben wandered into the cabin. He looked up into the open roof space, his eyes settling on the crumpled black plastic sitting on a timber slat toward the back of the cabin.

Ben pushed the door closed and crossed the floor. He climbed onto the workbench to get a better view. He would be quiet and get this over with quickly.

THE SECRET

He stood on his tiptoes and strained to see but he was too far away. Dad had used a chair to reach into the roof area, but Ben was not tall enough for that and the table looked too rickety to hold his weight.

Hungry.

So hungry. He had eaten a tiny morsel of the Kit Kat as they cleaned up the cabin but that was it.

He slipped down off the workbench and tried to push it but it wouldn't budge. He moved in behind it and put all his weight against it, shoving with everything he had. It moved a few inches, grinding across the wooden floor. He gave it another push, then crept to the door and looked out. No Dad. Mum still lying, lizardlike, on her rock on the opposite side of the clearing.

Ben rushed back across the cabin floor and pushed the workbench a few more inches. He stopped, listened, breathed hard, shoved it again. Another low wood-on-wood groan. He wondered if he'd be able to reach the plastic now but decided he needed to get at least a foot closer. He ran to the door and checked again, heart thumping lickety-split. Mum rolled over on her rock to face the cabin.

"What are you doing?" she called across the clearing.

"Nothing," he yelled back. "Just bored."

"Well, find something to do," she said, closing her eyes.

Olive was at the base of the tree now, still addressing her loyal subjects.

He ducked back inside. He would have to push the workbench across the floor in one almighty shove. It would be loud but otherwise it would take forever and Dad would return. He gripped the thick timber edges of the old bench, stretched one leg back behind him, and readied himself.

"One, two, three . . ." he whispered. The workbench screamed across the floor and came to a stop. So loud. He stood, breathless.

"Hi," said a voice. Ben's heart leaped from his throat. He turned to the door.

"*Shhh!*" he hissed at Olive. "Get out!"

She stood there, bottom lip out, then she pointed at him and screamed, "*You're mean!*" and ran away.

Ben eased the door closed. He heard Mum ask what had happened. He jumped up on the workbench, reaching as high as he could. His fingers managed to push the black plastic aside enough to scrape the bottom of something, but not quite enough to get a hold on it. He reached again and opened the plastic farther.

Ben recognized the bag as soon as he saw it. It was gray nylon with black handles. He positioned his toes on the very edge of the workbench and reached for the stars, pinching a corner of the nylon. He steadied himself and pulled at the tiny corner of material. He seized a handful of bag and lost balance, falling off the edge of the bench, pulling the bag down on top of him. Large clumps of something fell out.

Ben landed awkwardly on his side. One of the clumps that had fallen from the bag lay on the floor in front of his face, lashed together with a rubber band. Ben took it in his hand and sat up. A serious-looking man with a large forehead, thick eyebrows, and a bushy mustache stared back at him from the top of the pile he was holding. All around the man were pictures of cannons, soldiers, images of battle.

Ben was holding money. A lot of money. He had never in his life seen a single one-hundred-dollar bill. Now he clutched a wad of the green bills. He smelled it to see if it was real, but he had no idea what money was supposed to smell like. He flicked through it with his thumb. The pile of cash was two inches thick. How many hundred-dollar bills would fit into such a stack? Three hundred? Five hundred? Ben calculated it in his mind.

Could he really be holding $50,000? He glanced around and stood up to look in the bag, which lay twisted and open on the workbench. There were fifteen or twenty identical piles of cash in the bag and on the floor.

Dad and Mum never had spare money, even for shoes or haircuts. One of Dad's favorite sayings was "Money makes the world go round," but most of the time their world stood still. Ben had missed out on the science excursion on sand dune ecology a week earlier because they didn't have the fifteen dollars. But now they had lots of money. Why wasn't it in the bank?

A noise out front. Ben grabbed the sports bag and stuffed the thick blocks of cash back in, carefully watching the door and window. Fear roared through him, making him clumsy. He tried to shut the bag but the zipper was broken.

Dad said something to Mum. Ben's throat closed. He jumped up on the workbench and reached high, trying to shove the bag back into place, but he wasn't tall enough. He took steady aim and threw the bag onto the wide timber slat but it fell back into his hands.

"Where's the boy?" Dad called to Mum, his voice very near to the cabin now. Mum said something about Ben moving furniture.

He tried again, throwing the bag up onto the timber slat that ran across the roof beams. The bag held, but one end hung down, revealing the money. Dad's footsteps sounded on the gravelly sand near the cabin door. Ben jumped down, giving the workbench two tremendous shoves into position next to the wall just as Dad walked in. Ben breathed hard, guilt painted across his face in sweat.

"What're you up to?" Dad said. "Decorating?"

Ben took a slow breath and said, "Yeah. I tried moving things around but I reckon it all looks best where you had it."

Dad studied him for a few seconds. Ben took long, slow breaths.

"Can we go outside?" Ben asked.

"What for?"

"Explore . . . see the river."

Dad looked at him. "You sick? You never want to go outside."

"Yeah, but . . . there's all this nature."

Dad eyed him, walked to the table, grabbed his keys. "I've got to go out."

"Where to?" Ben asked, an awkwardly long time after his father had spoken.

Dad shook his head and looked at Ben, puzzled. "You're a very strange boy." He headed for the door.

Ben breathed out slowly and hope flooded in. He wished his father out of the cabin with everything in his soul.

Dad stopped in the doorway and turned, clicking his tongue like he had forgotten something. He looked up into the open roof space.

IN WHICH BEN GETS CAUGHT

Dad walked slowly to the back of the cabin, looking up, squinting to be sure that he could see what he thought he saw. A bag hung from the roof beam, a wad of cash lolling out like a tongue.

Ben crabbed sideways toward the door.

"Hey!" Dad called. It didn't sound like "Hey, you found my bag! I'd been meaning to tell you about the hundreds of thousands of dollars I'd hidden in the roof." It was more of a "Hey, you have about a second and a half before I explode like Vesuvius."

Ben stopped.

Dad turned and lunged at Ben, grabbing him by the scruff of the neck. He marched Ben to the back of the cabin and tilted his head up.

"*What* is this?" he barked.

Ben looked at the bag, hanging, threatening to fall.

"Is everything okay?" Mum called from across the clearing.

"Was this you?" Dad shouted at Ben, daring him to lie.

Ben was too scared to say anything. The neck of his shirt was pulled tight against his throat. Difficult to breathe. He heard running.

Olive arrived in the doorway.

"What happened?" Olive asked.

"You go climb the tree, sweetie," Mum said, arriving next to her.

"But I—"

"Go!"

Little footsteps.

Ben wanted to climb a tree too, for the first time in his life. Or to hide in his mum's skirt like he had when he was two.

"Was it you?" Dad asked.

"I didn't see what was in it," Ben said.

"What'd I tell you about stickin' your big bib in?"

"I don't know," Ben said.

Dad was quiet then. In Ben's experience it was never good when adults were quiet in this kind of situation.

"I think—" Mum said.

Dad shushed her.

"What do you think I should do?" he said, letting go of Ben's collar. Ben stood up straight, avoiding eye contact with his father. There was no correct answer to this question. Ben would either suggest a punishment worse than Dad had in mind or he would suggest something easier, nicer, and his father would erupt.

Ben shrugged, concentrating on his feet. His shoelaces were grubby and splotchy. One was untied. The leather on the toe and side of his right sneaker was gray and worn from soccer. Ben closed his eyes for a moment. On the movie screen at the back of his eyelids, he watched the last ten minutes of his life in rewind, like he was scanning back over one of his movies. He wanted to reshoot every frame from the moment he entered the cabin. He wanted to stay outside, not let curiosity get the better of him. He did not want to know what was in the bag.

"*What* do you think I should do about busybodies?" Dad said sharply, lifting Ben's chin, pressing "stop" on Ben's in-brain rewind. *"What?"* Dad shouted again.

"It's not his fault," Mum said, taking a few steps into the cabin. Ben could see her hovering behind Dad.

"What's not his fault? That I can't have a single thing to myself without someone sticking their nose into it?"

"We sold the wreckers," Mum said.

Everyone was quiet. Dad blinked and straightened his body, taking in what she had said.

"What?" Ben asked, turning to her.

"Dad. He sold the wrecking business."

Ben thought about this for a second. "Did they pay cash?"

Mum nodded and scratched her neck.

Ben looked at Dad, who stared back. "Well, why didn't—"

"We thought you'd be upset," Mum said.

"Upset?" Ben asked. Why would she say that? Mum knew that he didn't like the wrecking yard. It was filled with dead, broken, rusty things, and when he was there he had to search for parts or clean the toilet or restock the drinks fridge. The only good thing about the wrecking yard was when he found something interesting, like his camera, in one of the cars.

"Right," Ben said. "So . . . is the money . . ." He stopped. He tried to think back through the events of the past two days, but his thoughts were scrambled. He suddenly felt tired. "How long are we staying here?" he asked.

"I need to work out what we're doing," Dad said.

". . . for the rest of the vacation," Mum added.

"Yes, for the rest of the vacation," Dad said. "Get away from me. Go and play."

Ben did not need to be told twice. He slipped past his father, around his mother, grabbed his backpack from near the door, and exited the cabin. His parents began arguing. Ben walked to the edge of the steep hill and looked down through the pine forest toward the river. He had never spent time in the bush, had never left the suburbs. He did not want to go to the river. The wilderness was his enemy.

"What did you do?" said a voice from above. Ben looked up, squinting into the sun. It was Olive sitting on the lowest branch of the tree.

The hunger hit Ben again. It was lunchtime, and his stomach ached, but he knew there was no food.

"I'm goin' out!" Dad stormed out of the cabin. He was carrying the sports bag.

"Be careful, Ray," Mum said, following him. "And please make the arrangements today. I can't stay here."

Dad climbed into the car and slammed the door.

"Ray?"

"Yes, I'll make the arrangements," he said through the window.

"And get some clothes for the kids!"

Dad reversed, spun the wheel, and powered off up the hill, leaving them in a cloud of swirling dust.

Ben turned and, without a word, he let the trees take him. He let himself go off the edge of the slope and disappear. Down, down, down.

CULPAM POENA PREMIT COMES

Ben flew steeply down, dodging thick, rough chocolate-brown tree trunks, his feet deep in pine needles. Sun lit him in sharp bursts as he thundered into the valley. The water-rush became ever louder, filling him up.

The river emerged through the trees, and Ben began to slow, digging his heels into the damp black soil beneath. He came to a skidding stop at the large, mossy sandstone boulders that led down to the water. The river was about thirty feet wide. Sun hit the surface in patches, revealing muddy brown rocks beneath. Ben wondered how deep it was. Downstream there was a small waterfall leading to a lower section of river. On the far side, a sheer sandstone cliff soared a hundred feet above Ben's head. Fishbone ferns poked from cracks and scars in the cliff. The wall ran along the river's edge as far up- and down-stream as he could see.

Thirst tore at him then. He jumped onto a small boulder that was shaped almost like a pyramid and leaped from rock to rock, careful to avoid the slippery-looking patches of moss. He was halfway down to the water when he thought about snakes. They liked rocks. He had a book on snakes at home, a library book that he had never returned. (After snakes, his

greatest fear was ever going back to the public library, in case
he was arrested for theft.) Ben loved to scare himself in the
comfort of his bedroom, but out here he couldn't shut the book
and stop the fear. Nature was real and true and terrible.

He paused on a rock and looked up the hill, thinking of
running back to the safety of the cabin. Which was worse?
Snakes or his family? Fear told him to get off the rocks, but
thirst drove him down to the water. He pulled his school socks
up to his knees and stepped carefully, eyes darting all around,
waiting for venomous fangs to emerge from a crevice and end
him. He stepped onto a mossy green rock near the water, slip-
ping and breaking his fall with the palms of his hands. The
sting screamed, and he quickly dipped his hands into the fast-
moving river. The water was cold, soothing the sting. His
throat and stomach howled for liquid.

Ben looked upstream, wondering if the water was safe to
drink. He cupped water in his hands. There were tiny specks
of moss and other plant matter floating in it, but Ben's thirst
was too great. He brought the cupped handful to his mouth
and gulped it down. He scooped his hands in again and sucked
the water back into his throat. It felt so good and cold that
his head and insides lit up. He scooped again and slurped
thirstily, drinking water till his belly ached. He splashed his
face and collapsed back onto the mossy rock, another boulder behind him making a backrest.

There was something uncomfortable in Ben's back
pocket. He took it out. The book he had taken from the

cabin. *My Side of the Mountain.* Ben flicked through. There were illustrations showing how to make a trap for deer and a fishhook out of twigs. He read the back cover. It was about a kid named Sam Gribley who runs away from home in New York City to live in the Catskill Mountains by himself. He sleeps inside a tree and survives off the land. Ben threw the book onto the rock next to him. His eyes darted around. He knew that he would have no chance out here alone. Ben's survival skills included hunting for leftovers in the fridge, lowering bread into the toaster, and switching on the heater when it was cold. None of these talents would be useful here.

He breathed hard and sat up straight. He felt better, even with a bellyache. It was cooler down by the water. The moist, woodsy air and the steady *shhh* sound of the river seemed to swallow him and make him part of it all. Ben looked up through the ferns and spiky plants sticking out of the rocks, but he couldn't see the cabin.

"Mum," he called.

No response.

"Mum!"

The echo of his own voice off the rocks.

He was alone. Just Ben. And river and bird and frog. And snake.

He stood and lifted a palm-size rock and threw it into the river just to see the splash. He stuffed the book back into his pocket and grabbed another rock, throwing it as high as he could, the impact kicking splash all over him and putting a smile on his face for the first time in days.

As Ben turned to look for another rock he saw something move at the corner of his vision. It was a rabbit, a light gray one, hopping from the tree line to the top rock. It stopped, looked down at him, still. Ben began to move slowly up the rocks, but the rabbit skittered off the way it had come. He smiled again, looking all around. At home the closest thing he had to his own secret place was the crusty patch of land at the back of the wrecking yard. The tall grass there was peppered with graffiti-stained cars and the trains speeding by were loud and annoying. But here there was nothing man-made. Only Ben.

Why would Mum and Dad come out here just because they had sold the wreckers?

The money. So much money. He took his backpack off, pulled out his notebook, and sat down to jot the following sums:

$100 × 500 bills in bundle
= $50,000
$50,000
× 20 bundles
=

Ben stared at the page. There might not have been five hundred bills in a bundle but Ben figured there must have been close to that. And there might have been fifteen bundles, not twenty. But there could have been twenty-two. How could their old wrecking yard be worth a million dollars? The place was a disgrace. And if they did sell it for that much, why had Dad hidden the money? Why hadn't they told him about selling the business earlier? And who had bought it? Uncle Chris? Maybe. He had given Dad the bag full of money. Dad didn't even like Uncle Chris. Maybe that's why he sold it to him. Payback for all the beatings Uncle Chris gave him as a kid. Dad still had scars from Uncle Chris's babysitting sessions.

There were all these missing parts of the story. Adults never told kids anything. Nothing worth hearing anyway. Ben felt as though he spent his entire life trying to work out things that adults knew but wouldn't tell him. He would do some detective work, search for clues, put the puzzle together.

Ben pulled the police business card out of his notebook. "Dan Toohey." The wedge-tailed eagle emblem looked a bit like the bird on the front of *My Side of the Mountain*. Ben whispered the words *"Culpam Poena Premit Comes"* and decided that he would have his own police business card one day. One day when he was in charge of himself. He slipped the card back into the notebook. The river rushed by. Three birds, rosellas, flew past, chasing one another out over the river, then up into the trees. Ben flipped back a couple of pages and read:

Police
Vacation

Uncle Chris. Gray nylon bag. Black handles.
The new old car
Haircuts

He added:

Pulled over by cops. Drive off and chase.
The cabin
Bag full of money
Sold the wreckers

Sun emerged from behind the clouds. Bright splotches of light on Ben's notebook. He reread the notes. One thing was clear—weird stuff was going on. His parents were in trouble. He didn't know why, but he knew they were.

"What're you doing?" said a voice from above him.

Ben snapped his notebook shut.

MY SIDE OF THE RIVER

Ben leaped quickly from boulder to boulder, heading farther downstream, trying to get away from her.

"Leave me alone!"

"No. It was my idea to come down here," Olive said. "Then you just . . . poopsnaggled off by yourself."

"There's no such word as 'poopsnaggled.' Get a dictionary. And go away!"

"What were you writing?"

"Nothing."

"You wrote 'bag full of money' and 'sold the wreckers.' Who sold the wreckers?"

"Nobody," he said.

"Then why was Dad so cranky with you?"

Ben continued to make his way across the boulders on the riverbank, scanning the rocks for snakes.

"What did he hide in the roof?" Olive asked, struggling to keep up with Ben, jumping from rock to rock.

"Olive! *Go a-way!*"

"One day I'm going to steal your stupid notebook and read the whole thing and show my friends and laugh and—owww!"

Ben turned. Olive had slipped on a rock.

"Aaaaaarrrgggh!" she cried.

"Serves you right."

"He-e-elp, Ben!" She was lying, legs in the air, face twisted in pain.

Ben wanted to be strong and continue up the riverbank, but he couldn't. He sighed, made his way across the boulders, and helped her up. Her palms were scratched and stinging like his. He scooped his hands under her armpits and helped her down to the river.

"Dip them in the water," he said.

"No, it'll sting, you idiot!"

"Does it sting now?"

She looked at him for a moment, then slowly, carefully slipped her hands into the water.

"Ow," she said quietly.

"Is that better?"

She nodded and sniffled.

"You'll be okay," Ben said.

She took her hands out of the water and shook them.

Ben looked around. He massaged his hands together like he did when he felt creative. "You want to help me?"

"Do what?" Olive asked.

"I don't know. Build something maybe. Come on." He stood and helped her up to flat, dry ground. "Watch out for snakes."

"Where?" Olive said. "I love snakes."

Ben shook his head. He walked up to the edge of the pine trees. He found a long branch and dragged it down to the boulders. Olive saw another branch about the same length and picked up the end of it, grappling with it and struggling to drag it down the hill.

Ben had never built anything life-size before. Just his movie sets and characters. And half a model aircraft carrier with Dad when he was seven. Dad was always promising to finish it with him but he never did.

Ben and Olive searched for a long time, dragging together the best branches they could find. Most of them were straight and brown, about nine feet long, with a few twigs sticking out near the ends, which were easy to snap off. The branches had fallen from the tall pines above.

"Hoop pine," Olive said.

"What? How do you know that?"

"They look like the ones I saw in a book at school."

"Really?" he said. He liked the sound—"Hoop." He whispered the words "hoop" and "pine" as he worked. He noticed Olive quietly saying "hoop pine, hoop pine" to herself too. They became lost in searching and dragging.

After a time, Olive counted the branches.

"Sixteen!" she announced. "Six-teen branches. See! Count them. There's sixteen."

"I believe you."

"What can we build?"

Ben stopped and looked at their haul.

A fort?

Another cabin?

A tepee?

A raft.

The branches were almost laid out like a raft already.

"A raft," he said.

"Yes!" Olive said. "You're so smart. And we can take off and go discovering! And we'll be bushrangers! I'll be Olive Thunderbolt, pretend sister of Captain Thunderbolt, one of the most famous bushrangers of all time, and you can be Captain Thunderbolt and . . ." Olive went on to list all the good things about having your own raft, including plundering treasure and sailing the seven seas and saying "Arrrrrrr, me pretties" a lot. Ben tried to point out that bushrangers did not say "Arrrrrrr, me pretties," but she ignored him and said, "Olive Thunderbolt has a rosella sitting on her shoulder like a parrot and she's the driver of the ship. Captain Thunderbolt can be the first mate if he wants to be. Or a servant. When I grow up I'm not going to have a husband. Just a servant and a gardener."

Ben wondered what they could use to hold the raft together. He set off along the riverbank, Olive prattling happily next to him about a shipwreck and needing to fix the hull.

For the first time since they had arrived Ben started to relax. With just the two of them down by the river, it actually seemed a bit like a vacation. Ben wanted to go barefoot like Olive, but he was too scared of snakes.

He scanned the ground for long, thin vines that might work as rope to weave between the branches. Across the river there were vines snaking down the rock wall, but he would have to get to the other side of the river first. And, for that, he would need a raft. He could swim across, but the water was cold and running fast. He didn't know how deep it was, and he was not a good swimmer anyway.

They wandered for half an hour, the sound of water flowing by gently washing the past few days out of Ben's head.

"Imagine we're lost," Olive said, "and we've got to survive and we need to finish our raft so we can get food. And if we don't find food we've got to eat each other."

Ben smiled.

"I wouldn't really eat you," Olive said.

"Thanks."

"You'd taste disgusting."

Ben pinched her arm.

"Ow. What about that?" Olive said.

She was pointing at a clump of tall, tough-looking grass. Ben climbed onto a rock and jumped to the next, then pulled on a couple of the long strands. They did not budge. He pulled again, and his finger slipped along the sharp edge and opened up, bleeding. He sucked on the finger, swallowing the blood. He bent down low where the stem was round and white and juicy. He snapped it off, then gathered fifteen stems, passing them to Olive.

They ran along the bank, in and out of shadows, back to the branches, where Ben began winding the reeds through them. Up and over, down and under, up and over.

"Can you tell me now?" Olive asked.

"What?"

"Why you got in *trouble*," she said.

"Doesn't matter," Ben said.

"Does to me."

Ben thought about the money, about Dad's reaction. And his mother's lies. He knew the police had not come to their house over parking tickets. And he knew they had not sold the wreckers.

"Do you think Dad killed somebody and he was hiding the body up in the roof?"

"No!" Ben said. "Why would you say that?"

"Just joking," Olive said, smiling and doing a spin like a ballerina. "You're too serious sometimes, Benjamin."

"Don't call me Benjamin. And where do you hear stuff like that?" Ben asked. He tied another reed to the end of the first piece of grass and continued weaving it through the branches.

"At school," she said. "We play dead dog where you have to shoot a dog with a barrenarrow—"

"Bow and arrow," Ben corrected.

"Then you have to hide the dog somewhere in the playground and kids have to find it."

"Real dogs?" Ben asked, smiling.

"No. Pretend dogs. I usually choose a poodle because they're not very heavy. I picked a Labrador once and nearly died from dragging it over to the bushes behind the swings."

Ben wanted to ask how a pretend dog could be heavy and how the others find the dogs if they are invisible, but he could see the conversation going on for hours.

"So what was he hiding? Tell me or you're not coming to my birthday party."

"I don't want to come to your birthday party," Ben said. "And you're probably not having one."

"Yes, you do . . . And yes, I am!"

"No, I don't and no, you're not."

"Fine, I'm going on a cruise around the Caribbean, finishing up at Walt Disney World with a cake that has blue icing, but whatever."

Cake. Food. *Hunger.* Ben could taste the icing.

"Don't worry about it," he said. "It wasn't important. Just Dad getting angry like always."

He continued weaving reeds through the branches at four different points along the raft. It was slow work, but the shush of river and call of birds made them forget about time. After an hour they stood back and looked at their creation. Ben had used nine branches. It was a bit rough and wonky.

"Not bad for a first raft," Ben said.

They lifted the end of it and dragged it down over the slick rocks. The raft was heavy and awkward to carry, the center of it sagging. Ben worried that the grass ties might snap. He took three or four breaks before he was finally able to drop one end of the raft into the river. He sent a prayer up into the trees and sky that it would float.

There was a shrill whistle from up the hill.

"You two! Come!" Dad's voice echoed through the tall timbers.

"Olive? Ben?" Mum called. "Food!"

He wanted to pretend he didn't hear, but it must have been three o'clock and he was so hungry.

"C'mon," he said.

"I want to see if it floats," Olive whined.

"Later," Ben said. "We need to eat."

They dragged the raft up the rocks. Ben found some bushy branches and covered it.

"Ben!" Mum called again.

"Keep your pants on," he muttered, and started to make his way up the hill, Olive scrambling behind him. He could feel the river flowing out of his body, and fear flowing in. Would Dad still be angry about what Ben had seen? He used to think that there were two of his dad, the nice one and the angry one. Lately the nice one hadn't been around much.

As he climbed the hill, Ben made a promise to himself that he would work out where the money had come from and why they were lying to him. He was sick of being treated like a child. He was going undercover. He would find the truth.

KNIFE

Ben and Olive came over the rise and into the sandy clearing in front of the cabin, crossing back into the real world.

"Detective," Ben whispered, reminding himself.

"What?" Olive asked as they headed toward the cabin.

"Nothing. Don't tell them about the raft, okay?"

"Why not?"

"It's our secret." He stopped outside the cabin. Olive grinned. He knew that this would make her feel big and special. He didn't know why he needed it to be a secret, but he did. She probably wouldn't keep the secret, but he could hope.

Detective.

He pushed open the door.

"Here they are!" Dad said. He sounded almost chirpy.

Mum and Dad were seated at the table on new camping chairs. There was other camping equipment around the cabin—ice chest, blow-up mattresses, gas cooker. Ben dared to look into the open roof area. Dad had already taken the bag.

"You've been gone for ages," Mum said. "Thought you two were dead."

"No. Still alive," Ben said.

The table was filled with food. The sight and smell of it filled his mouth with saliva. Olive sat on a wooden crate. The only thing left for Ben to sit on was the small green metal trunk. He dragged it over and sat, grabbing at the food, filling his paper plate and stuffing crackers and cheese into his mouth.

"Slow down," Mum said. But she soon forgot, and they ate like a pack of wolves, swallowing food in great chunks, desperate to fill the empty space. They didn't speak until the tide of hunger had gone out and the sugar had reached their brains.

"Ooohhhhhhhh," Ben groaned.

"Good, is it?" Mum asked.

"So goooood," he said in a funny, croaky voice, and they all laughed. Even Dad.

Late afternoon sun fell in through the window. The cabin felt brighter than it had that morning. Dad reached into his pocket and banged a small box down on the table in front of Ben.

Ben looked at it and then up at his father.

"Open it."

Ben was suspicious. Dad wasn't known for buying presents. He left that to Mum. She even bought her own birthday presents. Ben picked up the box. It was small and plain and gray. Ben wondered if there was some kind of punishment or prank inside. He carefully opened a cardboard flap at one end and let the contents slide out onto his palm. A smile washed over his face. He clutched his fingers around it.

"Ray!" Mum said.

"What?" Dad asked, wiping mayonnaise from the corner of his mouth.

Mum clicked her tongue and shook her head.

It was a knife. Swiss Army. Red with a white cross. A serious one. Chunky, with metal sides that felt cold on his fingers. Ben flipped out a large blade, then another, smaller one.

"You think you can take care of it?" Dad asked.

Ben nodded. He flipped out a saw, a tiny pair of pliers, a corkscrew, scissors, a screwdriver, and some small, mysterious, pointy tools. He picked a tiny pair of tweezers and a toothpick out of the side of the knife.

"I want one!" Olive said, sticking her bottom lip out.

"Ah, for you . . ." Dad said, taking a large box out of one of the tall paper shopping bags sitting on the floor behind him. He gave it to Olive, and she did a dance, pretending to play electric guitar with the box. This was the first interaction between Dad and Olive in over a week.

Ben was mesmerized by his knife. When every arm had been folded out he sat and looked at his dazzling red, white, and silver spider. It was the best thing he had ever owned.

"What do you say to Dad?" Mum asked, closing up containers, clearing paper plates, throwing them into a plastic garbage bag.

"Thanks," Ben said without looking up. He was already thinking about the raft and how he could cut and saw it with his knife and make it sturdier and take off downstream.

He almost started talking about it but something stopped him. He needed to keep his secret world by the river for himself.

"Awesome!" Olive said. She was holding a skateboard with a blue plastic deck and red wheels. She had been asking for one since she was four. Ben wondered where she would ride it out here.

Dad reached into his pocket and placed another small box on the table. "My love," he said. Ben looked up. He had only heard his father call Mum "my love" once or twice. It sounded creepy and uncomfortable.

Mum turned from where she was crouched packing food into the ice chest. She stood, eyes wide, looking like a little girl. Dad snapped open the top of the box, and Mum's eyes kindled. She took what was inside and slipped it onto her finger. It was a ring with a diamond in it.

Mum flung her arms around Dad, kissing him all over the face a thousand times. Ben didn't really like watching his parents kiss.

"Do you realize that this is the first real present you've bought me in fifteen years?" Mum said. "I paid for dinner the first time we went out. Do you remember? I should have known it was a bad omen."

Dad pulled a face at her. "All right," he said, turning to the big bags on the floor again.

"What else?" Mum asked, admiring her ring.

"Look on the front seat," he said. She went outside, opened the car door, and gave a little shriek. Through the window Ben could see that she was holding two boxes.

Dad had bought other presents for Ben and Olive too. Clothes for each of them in various sizes, just to be sure. Shoes for Olive. For Ben, a robotic Lego kit and a *Mad* magazine. For Olive, a pirate outfit and a hot-pink remote control pickup truck that could drive across the sandy clearing out the front. She loved her skateboard best. She rode it round and round inside the cabin.

It felt more like Christmas than any Christmas Ben had ever known. For that moment, everybody was happy. The way things were meant to be, the way they were in movies. The way Ben always imagined other families being. Maybe better.

As dark closed in on the cabin, Dad decided to try lighting a fire outside, and they laughed at his pathetic camping skills. Only Mum managed to get a decent flame going.

Later, as Ben lay on his squeaky new air mattress in the darkness of the cabin, with a belly full of food and his parents outside laughing and talking, he wondered . . . if life was full of good things and presents and they were all happy, did it matter where the money had come from? Did it matter why his father had driven off from the police? Did it matter that his mum had lied to him? Maybe he was overreacting. Maybe they really did sell the wreckers. Maybe that old corrugated iron office building and the broken-down machinery and all those smashed-up cars were worth that much money. And that's how they got the presents. What if it could always be like this? A million dollars could buy a lot of happy.

DETECTIVE BEN SILVER

Ben's eyes half opened. He was cold and had no idea where he was. No roar of cars or semitrailers on the highway. No trains. No background hum of electrical tower.

His eyes adjusted to the darkness. He saw Olive lying on her air mattress next to his. Mum and Dad's voices trickled in from outside. Not laughing and chatting like they had been earlier. Arguing now. Ben had that knife-in-the-belly feeling that he got when they argued late at night. He lay in the dark, alert, listening. Olive sucked her thumb, making a quiet squeaking noise.

There were other sounds too, when Ben listened deeply. Crickets or insects. A frog somewhere. Scurrying in a tree and a screech from high above. Not silence but not sounds that he knew. The noise of trucks and cars and trains was comforting. Known, mechanical things. But here everything was unknown. The only familiar sound was the arguing.

"Why?" Mum asked.

"Because we have to sit tight. It won't be forever, but we can't just . . ." Dad lowered his voice. Ben could not hear the rest of what he said, but it was spoken with intensity and Mum responded fiercely.

"Please. Just. Listen to me," he heard Mum say. "I never feel heard!"

Ben crawled across his air mattress, crept to the window, peered out.

A near-full moon shone through the pines, and the white-sand clearing gleamed like silver. Mum and Dad sat on their camp chairs next to a few smoldering coals. Dad poked the coals with a stick, sending orange splinters of light shooting into the air. They continued to argue in low voices, silhouettes lined with moon-glow.

Ben worried sometimes that his parents would not be together forever. But he also worried that they *would* be together forever. He lay down on his mattress with a grunt, pulling the dark blue sleeping bag up to his neck. Like the fire, happiness had flickered and died. He looked around at the roof beams, the shelf with the food, the dark cupboard. This was the creepiest place he had ever slept. He felt a sharp bite on his elbow and thought of all the spiders that must be in the cabin with him. And ghosts. If he were a ghost he would hang out in this cabin. It was perfect for ghosts, just not for humans.

Ben lay still, watching, feeling, listening. He couldn't count the number of nights in his life that he had gone to sleep with his parents fighting. Too many. Even after all these years, he still got that feeling in his belly, waiting for Dad to get into the car and drive off, wheels spinning on the road. Ben wasn't a churchgoer, but on those nights he prayed that his dad would be okay. He would lie awake until he heard the car shake and rattle back into the driveway after midnight.

He listened for a while, but tiredness crept up on him little by little, covering him like a cloak. He tried to shrug it off but he was losing the battle. The sound of the river cut through the voices and other night noises. *"Shhhhh,"* it said, dragging him down.

I need to know.

These words came to him, and his eyes flickered open. No matter how many pocketknives he was given he still needed to know where the money had come from. He sighed and turned over. The mattress squeaked on the floorboards. He found a comfortable position and closed his eyes again.

What are they arguing about? Why do we have to "sit tight"?

Why couldn't he just be happy? Everything was good. Everything had been *great* all afternoon. *Let it go. They'll be fine in the morning.*

He rolled onto his back, arms folded across his chest.

"Shhhhh," said the river, but Ben fought it. He would find out. He would listen to their conversation. He would learn where they were heading, what they were doing.

Ben reached over the side of his mattress and felt inside his backpack. His hand touched a days-old pear from school. He laid the pear aside on the floorboards, then felt in the bag for his camera. He ran his thumbs over the buttons, switched it on, and placed it on the green metal trunk. He sat up and framed a wide shot of the cabin. It was very dark, but the camera was good in low light. He hit the "record" button, and the red light shone. He threw some clothes on top, covering the red light, and he sent out a prayer that he had enough battery to catch their conversation.

His head hit the inflatable pillow, and he tumbled into a dark well of sleep.

EVIDENCE

"Sometimes I wish we hadn't done it," Dad said.

Ben waited, his mouth dry. He pressed the video camera speaker to his ear, listening over the burble and swish of river. He sat on the bank, his back against a tree. He had escaped the cabin with his backpack and camera before anyone else woke. The sky grew orange, but the sun had not yet risen over the wall of sandstone on the other side of the river.

The picture on the camera's flip-screen was too dark to see, and the sound was low, so he kept the speaker pressed to his ear, swatting at mosquitoes on his ankles and neck.

"It's too late now. You got us in. You get us out," said Mum's voice.

"I hate this place."

"Welcome to the club," Mum said. "Why didn't you think about that before you drove us all the way up here?" Then, in a quieter voice, "What about the kids? What are they thinking?"

Sometimes the words weren't clear, but Ben filled in the gaps for himself.

"I didn't have a lot of time. And the kids're fine. They're *kids*."

"Just because—"

"As soon as we get the passports we go," Dad hissed.

More shuffling sounds. No speaking for a while. Ben listened with every cell, muscles tight, breath short. He wondered if he should scan forward. Someone lay down on an air mattress, and it squeaked softly on the floorboards in the background.

"Worst case, we can't get the passports, we go into the desert, somewhere that doesn't even exist."

"Great," Mum said. "Sounds fantastic. I've always wanted to live in the desert, Ray. If you're falling apart here imagine what you'll be like out there."

"Don't talk to me like that!" he snapped.

"I just wish you'd listened to me in the beginning."

Ben waited for a long time but there was nothing more. Just Dad snoring loudly. Mum must have elbowed him because the snoring stopped. Three short, sharp snorts. Then silence.

Ben scanned forward but that was it. He rested the camera on his lap and listened to it over again. He pulled his notebook and pencil from his backpack and wrote these words:

> *Wish we hadn't done it.*
> *As soon as we get the passports we go.*
> *Disappear into the desert.*

He reread the notes. Passports. That was the most important piece of evidence. Where were they going? Dad always said that he knew Australia was the greatest country on earth so why would anyone want to go anywhere else. Even when Ben pleaded to go on vacation to Fiji or New Zealand like some kids in his class, Dad said no. Ben ran his fingers over the words on the page. He figured that this was what a real detective would do—chew over the evidence, ratchet through the possibilities.

Maybe it was nothing. Maybe they really were just going on vacation. Maybe they were getting passports for Fiji or New Zealand and were only stopping in at the cabin for a few days on the way to the airport. Dad was probably joking about the desert. Ben let out a breath and bit his bottom lip. Sometimes he wished that his imagination wasn't quite so good. He could never walk down a dark hallway or put out the garbage or stay home by himself without thinking scary thoughts.

He went to his raft and uncovered it. He took one end in his hands and struggled down over the rocks, carefully laying it in the water. He crouched and crawled on board, floating at the shallow edge of the river. Water rushed beneath him. The raft wobbled. Some of the grass ties split with the pressure of his body so he shifted his weight, which made the back of the raft move away from the river's edge. He scrambled for balance.

The ties continued to split. Ben clutched the narrow branches like he was a baby and they were his mama. He fell into knee-deep water, standing quickly, the freezing river ejecting him. The raft was in the middle of the river now, drifting toward the far bank, where it would be swept downstream and over the falls.

Ben was not a strong swimmer. He moved from knee-deep to waist-deep water with a sharp in-breath, the cold pinching him. He waded until he was chest-deep, the force of the water pulling him forward. He pushed off a rock with his toes and surged toward the raft, reaching for the back left-hand edge with two fingers.

He caught it, clamped it with his thumb, and pulled back, getting a better grip with his other hand. He swam with everything he had, trying to drag the damaged raft back toward the boulders that stretched halfway across the river.

The relentless pull of water made Ben panic. He was losing the battle. Just as he decided he needed to let go of the raft or go over the waterfall, his foot touched a rock at the river's bottom. He dug in and pulled hard against the current and, finally, nudged up against the large, smooth, mossy boulders that reached out across the river. He hung on, breathing hard, feeling alive.

After a few minutes he began the difficult climb up the slippery rocks. At the top he collapsed, panting and wet. He laughed. His first attempt at building a raft, at building anything other than clay figures and miniature stop-motion sets, had been a disaster. He slapped at mosquito bites on his neck and face and arms.

Wish we hadn't done it.

Passports.

It. What did Dad wish they hadn't done?

Ben stood and hauled the loosely connected branches of his raft along the boulders and up onto the riverbank, dropping them next to his notebook and camera. He took the knife from his pocket, flicked out a blade, and cut the remaining grasses away. The knife was sharp and worked well. He headed off into the heavy shadow of the trees, and after a time he came across some tough, rootlike vines growing along the ground at the base of a hoop pine. They would do.

The raft needed bracing, something going across to hold the longer branches together. Ben remembered this from a school excursion to the maritime museum in third grade. He'd seen a giant raft that had been across the Pacific Ocean. It had a sail and cross-bracing.

He worked as sunrise turned to daylight, wondering if the physical work and the hunger were making him any less fat. He hoped so. Nobody called for him, and he heard no other human sounds for a long time. He sawed a branch into three equal lengths, gnawing away at it with the tiny saw blade on his knife. He carved grooves in the longer branches and laid the shorter pieces across to brace the raft. He lashed his new raft together with the vines, working quickly, his body moving constantly to keep the mosquitoes away. They ate his ears and ankles for breakfast.

It.

Wish we hadn't done it.

Sold the business? Ben wanted to believe it, but he couldn't. He knew how much his parents hated the wrecking business. They'd started losing money the second Dad bought it.

Ben had done well to record their conversation, but now he needed to discover where the money came from, why they needed passports, where they were going. He needed to interrogate his father, to pry and uncover more evidence. He had somehow become a detective years before he ever expected to. It was scarier and less fun than he had imagined.

He pulled a vine tight and knotted it. The raft was finished.

Bang!

He ducked, pressing himself into the rough bark of his raft. He had never heard a real gunshot before, but that was what it sounded like.

THE HUNT

Ben watched, eyes alert, pupils black and big as marbles, glaring through the gloom of the pine forest. His father skulked through the trees higher up the hill, kicking pine needles and turning over rotting logs with a brown-booted foot. He twitched and spun at the slightest sign of movement. He was carrying the rifle from the cabin.

Ben had played millions of hours of games, and he wouldn't have thought that seeing a person with a real gun would bother him, but it did. Dad seemed nervous and unnatural with it. Ben wondered if he had ever held a gun before. He didn't seem to be holding it the right way. Not that Ben knew what the right way was.

He wanted to call out from behind the tree but he was struck silent. He thought of his camera and notebook and bent down to gather his things, throwing the notebook into his backpack and slinging it over his shoulder. He turned the camera on, hit "record," and poked the lens out from behind the tree. What was Dad hunting for?

Me. That was the answer that came to him. But the voice came from the same part of Ben's mind that told him to run when he was walking back from the bathroom in the middle of the night. It was the same part of his mind that his stories came from. The fear place.

Dad zigzagged down the hill, about ninety feet away. Ben kept the camera trained on him. Dad tucked himself in behind a large fallen tree and crouched. He pointed the rifle out into the forest, deadly still. Something moved to his right. *Bang!* Another shot and the movement was gone.

"Dad!" Ben called without thinking, training the lens on his father. Dad turned. Ben put a hand out from behind the tree in surrender and lowered the camera. Dad shook his head. He motioned silently, impatiently, for Ben to come toward him. Ben wanted to cover his raft but he was afraid of bringing attention to it, so he left it lying there on the ground between the tree line and the river. Ben tucked in beside Dad at the fallen tree. It was crawling with green ants.

"What are you doing?" Dad whispered.

"Just . . . hangin' around," Ben said.

"What time'd you get up?"

"Early."

"Well, you're lucky you're still alive, scaring me like that."

Ben stared at the rifle in Dad's hands. He couldn't help it.

"Did you fix it?" Ben whispered. The weapon was made of dark brown timber, black metal.

"Got some stuff for it yesterday down the coast. Cleaned it up this morning."

"Have you ever used one before?" Ben asked.

Dad shrugged. "Can't be that hard. Your pop used it."

"Did he ever show you how?"

"No," Dad whispered.

"Why are we whispering?" Ben asked.

"Rabbits," Dad said. "You seen any?"

Ben thought about the light gray rabbit he had seen the day before at the river. He shook his head. "Nope."

"I saw one just up there," Dad said, pointing. "Gray. Missed it. Ran off. Waiting for it to come out again."

They sat, quietly waiting for rabbits. Ben hoped that the rabbit was way underground, settling in for a bunch of carrots and a long nap. He wondered where rabbits would find carrots around here. He looked at the gun, Dad's grubby hands gripping it.

"Why do people shoot rabbits?" he asked.

"Eat 'em," Dad said. "They're a pest."

"Olive's a pest and we don't eat her," Ben said.

Dad looked out over the bumpy bark of the fallen tree in front of them, dirty blue cap with the gas company logo sitting limply on his head. He had creases and blackheads around the edges of his eyes. He looked more like a dog than a rat today, Ben thought. He wondered if dogs had hair growing out of their noses like Dad did. He couldn't remember ever seeing a dog with nasal hair.

Passports.

Ben wanted to ask why they needed them. He could say that he'd overheard his parents talking last night, but Dad would get angry. Ben did not want to anger a man with crow's-feet, nose hair, and a gun. He would have to be smart. He squeezed his bottom lip. *Interrogate,* he thought. *Get him talking.*

"I love it here," Ben said.

"Really?"

"Yeah." Ben was only partly lying. He liked being at the river by himself.

Dad raised his brows.

"Do you?" Ben asked.

Dad thought about it, adjusted his cap. "No. I don't."

"Why not?"

"Keep your voice down," Dad said, annoyed.

Ben asked again. "Why not?"

"I just don't," he said. "Your grandfather planted these trees thirty years ago. Thought a pine forest would make him rich. He thought a garlic farm would too. But he died poor."

"Is that why you don't like it here? Because of Pop?"

"No. I just like hot showers and cold beer."

Ben saw his chance. "So why don't we leave?"

Dad looked at him and then back to where he thought the rabbit was hiding.

"We will," he said.

"Go home?" Ben asked.

Long pause. "Not necessarily."

"Where then?"

"I don't know," he said.

"A long way away?"

"Too many questions, Cop," Dad said, a note of warning in his voice.

Ben stayed silent for a moment as the tension drained away, down the hill and into the river.

"I was just asking," he said.

"Well, don't 'just ask.'"

What would a detective do? He knew what he wanted Dad to tell him—where they were going next, why they needed passports. He just needed the questions that would unlock the answers.

Ben closed his eyes for a moment, concentrating. The curtains opened on the movie screen at the back of his eyelids. He imagined Ben Silver, Sydney's toughest cop, the hero from his movie, cross-examining Dario Savini, zombie thief. Ben Silver needed to get a confession of Savini's crime without being infected and turning into a zombie himself. Ben wasn't sure if zombies could speak, but in this part of his movie, they could. What would Ben Silver ask?

"How did you get like this?"

"Like what?" Savini would say.

"Like this. Don't you want a normal life—kids in school, soccer on weekends, a regular job?"

"I don't have a choice," Savini would say.

"Everybody has a choice," Silver would respond, thinking of his own beautiful wife, his Labradoodle, his two children, Gareth and Martha, both with clean clothes and perfect teeth.

"I am who I am," Savini would say. *"I'm a monster."*

"Open your eyes," Dad whispered.

Ben did.

"What were you doing?"

"Nothing," Ben said, adjusting slowly to the real world like he was walking out of a movie theater. Candy bar, popcorn machine, people lining up to buy tickets. Only here it was damp woods, green ants on fallen tree, father holding rifle.

"You said, 'I'm a monster,' " Dad told him.

"Sorry," Ben said, making a mental note not to say lines from his movies aloud when he was watching them on the secret movie screen behind his eyelids.

"Why do we need passports?" Ben asked.

Dad turned to him, finger tightening around the trigger. "What'd you say?"

Birds played chase. A gust of wind soared up through the valley.

Ben shrugged and looked out into the trees.

"Where did you hear that?" Dad asked.

Ben licked his lips with a dry tongue. "Did you and Mum do the wrong thing?" he asked. *Stop,* said his mind. *Stop speaking.*

"What makes you say that?"

"Just. Things don't seem normal. They seem . . . weird. That's all."

"Why would you think we would do the wrong thing?" Dad asked.

Ben shrugged. Dad's face turned a pale shade of red.

"Are we good people?"

Ben nodded, looking into his father's watery hazel-brown eyes. Cloudy, not clear. More like a dam than a lake.

"Do you think we're good people?" Dad asked again.

I hope so, Ben thought. He remembered Olive suggesting that Dad was hiding a body in the roof of the cabin.

"Yes," Ben said, unconvincingly. "I think we're good people."

"Then why would we do something wrong? And why did you ask about passports?"

A thick Y-shaped vein stuck out on Dad's forehead. Ben's backpack felt hot and heavy, the air tight and warm in his throat. Just then he saw a flicker of gray over Dad's shoulder and up the hill.

Dad must have seen Ben's eyes move. He turned quickly, raised the rifle, and took aim.

"Don't!" Ben said.

The rabbit's ears pricked up.

"Bang," Dad whispered.

NOTEBOOK

Dad sawed back and forth on the rabbit's left hind ankle with an old fishing knife. It made a *hawk*ing sound, like a dentist sawing a tooth. Then the foot came away, and he held it out for Ben, who stepped back toward the fire that Mum was trying to start.

"What? It's good luck," Dad said.

It didn't look like good luck to Ben. He wondered who came up with the idea that rabbits' feet were good luck. Surely they were better luck if they were still attached to the rabbit. Imagine if rabbits decided that human feet were good luck, so they started sneaking down chimneys and through cat flaps and gnawing off people's feet in the night. Apart from a foot being an extremely heavy thing for a rabbit to carry around, there would be millions of us walking around on our ankles.

Ben looked down at the rabbit. It was lying on its side on a low tree stump at the edge of the clearing. Dad was using the stump as a chopping block. The rings of the tree, stained with blood, seemed to radiate out from the rabbit. The one brown eye that Ben could see looked alive, but the rest of the animal was floppy and lifeless.

Dad poked the foot at him again, and Ben looked into his father's eyes. They seemed less alive than the rabbit's. The Y-shaped vein stuck out on his forehead again.

"No thanks," Ben said.

Dad shook his head. It was a shake that Ben had come to know meant "What's wrong with ya?" or "Big baby."

"I'll keep it myself then," Dad said with a grin, and he stuffed the bloody foot into his pocket. "Let's cook Bugs Bunny up. I'm hungry."

Ben watched his father. "Why are we eating rabbit? We've got real food inside."

Dad did not respond.

Ben slumped down against a nearby tree as Mum tried to help Dad gut and skin the rabbit. Mum and Dad bickered as Dad made mistakes. Eventually Mum took over. Olive hid in the cabin. She had decided when she was three that she was vegetarian and had not willingly eaten meat since. Mum had once tried to trick her by hiding chicken in a pie with lots of vegetables, but when Olive found out she refused to eat anything but crackers for a week.

Ben sketched the rabbit as he had seen it on the tree stump—the glistening brown eye, the tree rings radiating out from its body. He had never really thought that much about where meat came from before, about the process of an animal becoming food. Did it become meat as soon as it died or only once it was ready to be cooked? Or was it always meat?

Am I meat? he wondered. Ben squeezed his bicep. *Maybe I am,* he thought. *I hope they don't eat me.* Somehow, in supermarkets, the fluorescent lights and the shiny, plastic-wrapped packages made you forget.

Dad put the rabbit on a stick and held it over the fire. Or over the smoke, really. There weren't any flames. Just some warm sticks that he kept prodding and blowing on and trying to spark into life. He sat on the edge of the chopping stump, turning the rabbit occasionally, watching Ben. "What do you write in that book?"

"I'm not writing," Ben replied.

"What do you *draw*?"

"Just stuff."

"Where'd you get it?" Dad squinted as the wind changed and smoke blew into his eyes.

"It was Pop's."

Dad snorted. He had always acted strange when Pop's name was mentioned, even though Pop had been dead for years. He had died when he was fifty-six and had become a mythical figure, frozen in time. The stories about him became bigger each year: the way he helped people and gave his money away to friends who needed it. And how he did electrical work but didn't bother charging his customers. Nan said the only people that Pop had never had enough time for were his sons.

The curling smoke changed direction again, and Dad eyed Ben for a while but didn't say anything more.

Ben was starving. His father had already said he wasn't allowed to eat anything until the rabbit was cooked. When he was finished drawing he wrote down the interrogation scene that he had imagined between the Ben Silver in his movie and Dario Savini, zombie thief.

> BEN
>
> *How did you get like this?*

> DARIO
>
> *Like what?*

> BEN
>
> *Like this. Don't you want a normal life—kids in school, soccer on weekends, a regular job?*

> DARIO
>
> *I don't have a choice.*

> BEN
>
> *Everybody has a choice.*

> DARIO
>
> *I am who I am. I'm a monster.*

It was another hour before Dad announced that lunch was ready. Ben looked up from his writing, his back still against the hoop pine. The last thing he wrote, in big letters, in the middle of a page, was:

> *Can your own parents kidnap you? I think mine have. Help!*

Dad held up the rabbit on a stick—a charred black lollipop of meat. Then he took to it with a knife.

"Come try this," he called, offering Ben a lump of burned rabbit. Ben didn't know which body part it was, but it did not look good.

"I'm all right," Ben said. He was trying to sound tough and manly while still refusing to eat the meat. He didn't like it when Dad said he wasn't tough enough.

Dad smiled and bit into the rabbit himself, smothering his teeth and lips in charcoal.

"Good eating," Dad said, but even from fifteen feet away, Ben could tell that it looked red-raw on the inside. Dad jawed on it with his side and rear teeth, twisting the meat around and around.

"Tastes like turkey. There's scrub turkeys around here too, y'know."

Perfect, Ben thought. *Let's eat them too. Anything that moves, let's eat it.*

"Come on, everyone," Mum said. She had spread out a couple of towels close to the fire for them to sit on and was laying out tomatoes, lettuce, and bread. "Olive!" she called.

Olive appeared at the cabin door and took a wide arc across the clearing, as far away from Dad and the rabbit-fail as she could. She sat on a towel as Mum buttered bread for sandwiches.

Dad brought the meat over, carved up on a paper plate. He sat on a camping chair next to the towels and put the plate with the other food.

"Ray, that's not cooked," Mum said.

"Yes, it is."

"No. It's not. It's disgusting. You've spent nearly three hours preparing and cooking that and look at it."

"Oh well. Don't have any. All the more for me," he said. But he didn't eat any more right away, and Ben saw him drop the gristly piece that he had been chewing to the ground when he thought no one was looking. At home Golden would have snapped it up. Ben missed her.

Dad wiped charcoal off his lips, and the others made lettuce and cheese sandwiches. As Ben reached for a slice of tomato Dad snatched his notebook up off the towel, tearing some of the pages.

"Let's have a look at this," he said.

Ben turned, dropped the tomato, and grabbed for the book. "No."

Dad pulled it out of Ben's reach. "I want to know what you spend all your time writing in your little book. Wonder if there's anything about passports?"

"Give it to me." Ben's mind raced with the things he had written in there, the evidence he had gathered. He lunged for Dad, who palmed him off and stood, walking back a few steps.

He cleared his throat. "Very interesting."

"Give it back to him, Ray," Mum said.

Ben stood and followed Dad to the other side of the fire pit.

"Zombie thief, eh? Oh, and a little poem. How sweet. My son, the poet." He flicked roughly through the pages.

"Give me it!" Ben said in a low, threatening voice. He threw himself at Dad, who shoved him away.

"Just give it to him," Mum said. "He should be allowed some privacy."

"Hang on," Dad said, backing off again. "What's this? 'Pulled over by cops.' 'Bag full of money.' 'Sold the wreckers.' It's a diary too."

Ben ran at his dad and tackled him to the sandy ground near the smoldering fire pit. He wanted to stop but he couldn't. He grabbed at the notebook like a wild animal, screaming as Dad tried to get away, but Ben wouldn't let him. That notebook was the one place Ben could be himself.

"Ben! Don't," Mum said, standing. "What are you doing?"

"Ben!" Olive squealed.

Dad grabbed him by the arms and twisted his body, rolling him over and pinning him to the ground, sitting on his stomach. The notebook lay on the sand. "Don't you *ever* do that to me again, you hear?" Dad shouted, spit flying from his mouth. Ben struggled against his father's grip. Tears stabbed the backs of his eyelids. Dad gave a final, firm push down on his arms, then stood. Ben rolled and reached for the torn notebook, but Dad was too quick, sweeping it up off the ground.

"I don't know what you know, but I'm about to go and have a good read of this and find out. Keep your nose out of other people's business!"

Dad headed toward the cabin. A deep growl spewed from Ben's mouth, and he stood to give chase, but Mum ran over, intercepting him, holding him across his chest. "It's okay," she said, her voice shaking and breaking. "Let it go. Let him have it."

"You are the worst father in the whole *world*," Ben shouted.

"Boohoo!" Dad said as he disappeared inside the cabin, slamming the door.

Ben breathed hard, then screamed into the tall trees above. Everything he had written, all his thoughts and the evidence he had gathered in the past few days. He silently cursed what an idiot he had been to write everything down and to leave it lying around. Ben had no idea what his father would do once he had read the notebook, and he did not want to find out.

TRAPPED

Ben ground his teeth as the dream thundered through him. In his mind's eye he was at the river floating on his raft. He looked across the smooth water to find something watching him from the bank. He kept his eye on the face of the thing as he bobbed gently up and down. The wolf had his father's eyes, and it stole quickly into the water. Ben began paddling as the animal swam quickly to the edge of the raft. He crawled to the far side to get away, but the raft tipped. He fell in, panicked, and began to swim. He soon felt a slicing, twisting pain in his left calf. He kicked and fought the wolf, but it was too strong. He could not overcome it. Would never. As water filled him, he felt a hand on his shoulder.

"Where's Mummy?"

Ben's eyes jerked open. He heaved air into his lungs.

"Are you okay?" Olive asked, leaning over him. It was light outside. The cabin was hot. He looked to Mum and Dad's empty mattresses.

He sat up.

"The door's locked, and the car isn't there," Olive said.

Ben stood and trampled awkwardly over his mattress toward the window. She was right. No car.

"What do you mean it's locked?" he asked, stepping over Mum and Dad's mattresses. He pulled the door handle. It moved a little but did not open, which was impossible because Dad had broken the lock on the night they arrived. Ben pulled hard, and something clanked outside but it would not shift.

"They must have gone to get breakfast," Olive said.

Ben looked at all the food stocked up on the shelf.

"Yeah. Maybe." Ben searched around for a note from Mum. She always left a note. He lifted up the mattresses to see if it had slipped underneath. He shook out the sleeping bags.

He tried the door again. It flexed and jangled. A chain. A thick chain. Probably the one Ben had found when they were cleaning out the cabin. He walked back to the window and twisted the rusty metal latch. He hooked his fingers through the two metal rings at the bottom of the window and pulled upward, feeling a thick Y-shaped vein form on his forehead. But the window was jammed and swollen from years without use.

"Maybe Dad took the car and Mummy's gone to get water at the river. Maybe she'll be back in a minute," Olive said.

Ben thought of yesterday, when he had stood up to his father. He had asked too many questions when they were out hunting. He knew too much. And he had written it all down.

He had been sent to the cabin after Dad had finished reading his notebook. He had not been allowed out for dinner and had gone to bed hungry. Apart from the food he had stolen from the shelf when no one was looking. "Let's call out," Olive suggested.

"Okay," said Ben.

"Mu-u-u-um!" She listened for a few seconds. "Mum!"

Nothing.

"Mum-my!"

She waited.

"Help me!" she snipped at Ben.

So he gave a halfhearted call. "Mum!"

"Mu-u-m-m-y-y-y!" Olive screamed.

They listened. Ben looked around. It was dark inside. It was always dark in the cabin until late afternoon, when the sun would find a gap in the trees for half an hour. Ben eyed the high, broken window in the open roof area. It would be near impossible to get to. Too small for him to squeeze through and probably too small for Olive. Broken glass hung from the top of the frame like stalactites.

Hungry.

Ben was not sure what time it was but it felt late, nine o'clock he guessed, much later than his usual wake-up. He wished he was at Nan's, eating cookies out of her tall yellow cookie jar. He didn't care how much cat fur was in among the cookies or if there were weevils. He wanted to tell her everything while she drank a big cup of tea from her purple mug. She would know what to do. She always knew.

"Where are they? And why is the door locked?" Olive asked.

"I don't know," Ben said. But he did know. He knew that his parents had not sold the wreckers. This was not a vacation. The police wanted them for some reason, and Ben's sloppy detective work had led to him and Olive being held captive.

Ben spied the ice chest in the corner of the room and lifted the lid. Ice, cheese, tomatoes, juice, cold meat wrapped in white paper, all floating in icy water at the bottom. He grabbed a large block of chocolate and shook off the water. He unwrapped it and snapped off a row. Caramel.

He looked at it, wondering if he should eat it. How much fatter would it make him? How delicious would it be? He could hear his mother's voice: "It's your choice. Don't blame me," and he could hear the things kids sometimes said at school when they were picking teams for soccer. Ben was always goalie. "You just have to stand there and block the goal with your body," they would say, laughing. Ben would laugh along too, but it wasn't that funny. And he remembered when the school had sent home BMI report cards—Body Mass Index. It was the only report where he had scored really high marks.

Ben shoved the chocolate into his mouth.

Knowing that it was Dad's made it taste especially good. He devoured the row, then another. He offered some to Olive. She shook her head, bottom lip out, arms folded.

Ben munched on another row, caramel spilling down his chin. Olive grunted. Her body stiffened.

"What's wrong?"

She turned her back to him.

"Are you angry at Mum and Dad?"

She didn't say anything. Ben put a hand on her shoulder. Tears spilled down her cheeks as she buried her head in his side. He wanted to say, "Don't be a baby," but Olive never cried unless it was serious.

"Just Mummy," she said, muffled by sobs.

"You're just cranky at Mum?"

She nodded and howled to herself.

"Why?"

"Because Dad's a big Maugrim-ish idiot, but Mummy knows better than to be mean and bad."

Ben held her for a few minutes, warm tears making the side of his T-shirt soggy.

"At least we can eat Dad's chocolate," he said. He snapped off another row and offered it to her. She took it and ate it quickly, then asked for another. Ben wondered if he was already fatter.

He looked around the room, sighing. He had his new Lego and knife and other presents from Dad, but he didn't feel like using any of it. He had not seen a screen in days. Back in real life he watched TV, made movies, or played games from three-thirty in the afternoon till nine at night. They always ate dinner in front of the TV. Dad would get angry if anyone tried to eat at the dining table when a good show was on. He said it was rude. When Ben stayed at James's house, they didn't even have a TV, which was odd. And Gus was only allowed to watch it on weekends. But to Ben's family, TV was like bad glue. They needed regular doses to keep all the cracks hidden.

The roof of the cabin clicked and creaked, expanding in the sun. Rosellas made a mad tweeting racket in the pine trees behind the cabin.

"I need to go to the bathroom," Olive said.

Ben needed to go himself. He leaned the air mattresses up against the wall and paced around the cabin, squeezing his bottom lip. How long would his parents be gone? Too long for Olive.

"Where can I go?" she asked. "I'm going to explode!"

Olive went from not needing to go at all to nearly exploding every time. It drove Dad crazy, especially when they were driving.

Ben heard the river in the distance, and for a moment it seemed to flow through him, making him feel as though he might explode too.

"We have to smash the window," Olive said.

"No! Go in a cup." Ben moved quickly to the shelf and grabbed a plastic cup out of the packet.

"I'm not a boy! I can't go in a cup," she said.

Ben had already thought about smashing the window, but what if his parents really had gone to get breakfast? What if Dad was coming back with bacon and eggs on rolls and strawberry milk to apologize for reading Ben's notebook?

"We can't smash the window. They'll kill us," he said.

"Well, I'll already be dead from an exploding bowel."

"Bladder."

"What?"

"Pee is held in your bladder."

Olive punched Ben hard on the arm. "They can't just lock us in. Kids are people too." She picked up a saucepan and went to the window.

"Don't!" Ben said. "They'll be so angry."

"They're gone!" Olive shouted. "They've left us to be eaten by lions and possums and . . ."

"No, they haven't. Possums can't eat you, and there are no lions in Australia."

"We saw—"

"*Except* at the zoo," Ben said.

"Well, what if they escaped?" she said, raising the pan over her shoulder.

"*Stop!*" Ben grabbed her arm. "Let's . . ." He tried to think of something to distract her.

"Why don't we play with your remote control truck?"

"No."

"Skateboard?"

"No!"

"Let me tell you a story. It'll take your mind off it."

"Let me go or I'll bash you with the saucepan."

"Do you promise not to smash the window?"

"Let. Me. *Go!*" she screamed, and he dropped her wrist. "What about?"

"What?"

"What's the story about?"

The saucepan hung by her side, threatening to rise again if Ben didn't come up with something good. He searched the room for inspiration. His backpack lay on the floor next to his camera and the torn notebook. Dad had thrown it at Ben after reading it and told him that his detective work sucked.

Ben could tell her the story of Dario Savini, zombie thief, and Ben Silver, Sydney's toughest cop, but it seemed a bit creepy. The ancient, dog-eared copy of *My Side of the Mountain* sat, cover up, on the floor near his notebook.

"How about a story about a kid who has to survive in the wilderness by himself, living in a tree."

Olive dropped the saucepan to the floor with a *clang* and sat on one of the camping chairs, thumb in her mouth. She and Bonzo waited.

Ben breathed a stuttering sigh and picked up the book. He climbed onto the table, leaning his back against the wall next to the window. He began to read the author's note at the beginning—how when she was a kid she had packed up a suitcase and told her mother she was going to run away from home.

Over the next few hours, Ben started to unravel the story of Sam Gribley, the kid who left home to live in the mountains with only a weasel and a falcon for company. As he read the book aloud his mind pedaled furiously in the background.

I hope it wasn't me who sent them away, with all my stupid evidence and notes. They'll come back for sure. They'll be back by lunchtime. I know they will.

HOLE

Ben worked the small, jagged blade back and forth across the floorboard. He was starting to make a decent groove now. As he worked he listened for the sound of a distant engine, but there was nothing.

"Shine it over here," he said.

Olive focused the flashlight beam on Ben's work. Rain hammered the old tin roof.

They had read *My Side of the Mountain* in two sittings, one before lunch and one after. They had taken turns to read aloud and had finished the book by flashlight as the sun abandoned them for the day. Ben had never loved reading. He liked movies or a teacher reading them a book, but he did not like wading through millions of words alone. But this book played on the movie screen in his mind, like when he imagined his films. No one was showing him pictures but he could still see them.

Olive had peed in the cup. She had made Ben turn his back and reminded him of the time that he made her drink apple juice. Well, he had told her it was apple juice but it was not. It was something else. Something that *looked* like apple juice, but he had made it himself. Ben laughed but he still felt bad.

Why did he do those things to her? It was as though there was a bad-Ben inside him, forcing his hand.

My Side of the Mountain had given them comfort and light and warmth, but when it was done all they had was heavy rain, leaks spattering the floor around them, and small, unseen animals making nests in the darkest corners.

After dinner Ben had said, "Let's get some sleep. Tomorrow, this day will feel like a dream. They'll be here when we wake up, you wait."

"Liar," she had said, darting across the cabin to grab her saucepan and heading for the window.

"Stop. We don't want to be out there at night. And we don't want to smash anything. Think what Dad will do." Ben had already been thinking about a way out of the cabin that would not get them into too much trouble if Dad came back. And if they really had been abandoned, they needed to be able to come and go without smashing a window. "Why don't we cut a hole in the floor, something we can cover up. A trapdoor."

"I love trapdoors," Olive had said.

"I know that."

She lowered the saucepan. "What do we cut it with?"

Ben had pulled his knife out of his pocket, shoved the small, rusty green metal trunk across the floor. He had run his fingers over the pine floor, found a small knothole about a foot away from the wall, and started to cut away at the board.

"That'll take ten years!" Olive had said. "Lemme smash the window."

It did take a long time to get going, and the blade stuck regularly in the wood, but Ben was determined. Olive held the flashlight, but her mind wandered and so did the flashlight beam.

"This is payback for those dirty dogs leaving us," she said.

Ben moved the blade back and forth, back and forth. *Dirty dogs. Dirty dogs.* Those words sawed through him. *Dirty* on the forward motion of his saw. *Dogs* on the backward. The more he thought, the more he sawed, the more he became certain that he and Olive needed a way out, that maybe Mum and Dad were gone for good. But why would they do that? Why would they lock Ben and Olive in?

"Do you think he's real?" Olive asked, sitting above Ben on a camp chair.

"Who?" Ben asked. *Dirty dogs. Dirty dogs.*

"Santa."

Ben stopped sawing. He looked around the dark room. "Who said anything about Santa?"

"Just me."

Ben started sawing again. "Yes. He's real."

Olive was quiet.

"Do you think kids in Africa are dying right now?"

"Maybe," Ben said. "I guess so."

"Are other kids in Africa getting born?"

"Yeah. Of course."

"Why don't kids in Africa get Christmas presents?"

"They do," Ben said, wiping sweat off his face with his shoulder.

"No, they don't."

"How do you know?" Ben wanted to work in silence, but at least the chatter stopped him from thinking about Mum and Dad and what they had done.

"Movies," Olive said. "In Christmas movies Santa never goes to Africa."

"Really?" he asked, surprised. He tried to think of one where they did.

"Mm-hm," Olive said, sucking her thumb now while holding the flashlight.

Ben blinded himself for a moment by looking into the flashlight beam.

"Stop sucking your thumb."

"You're not my dad."

No. And you wouldn't listen to me if I was.

Ben felt the saw go all the way through the timber for the first time.

"Give me the flashlight!" he said, blowing sawdust aside. He lay down and put his eye to the crack, trying to squeeze the flashlight as close to his eye as he could. Through the tiny slit, Ben could see corrugated iron on the ground and lots of old bottles. This pinprick of hope pushed him up off the floor, and he worked double time, hacking away like his life depended on it. And maybe it did. He would have to cut through three floorboards to make a hatch wide enough to escape. His hand ached like when he was forced to write for a long time at school, but it was easier now that he could push and pull all the way through the board. After almost an hour he had cut across an entire floorboard. He pried it up, and the rusty nails near the wall bent and twisted and the board came away.

"Ya-a-a-a-a-y!" Olive said, shining the flashlight into the gap. Ben used the piece of floorboard to scrape away the twisted mass of spiderwebs beneath and reached his arm down into the outside world, laughing for the first time that day. Breeze. He could almost touch bare earth.

"Let me, let me!" Olive said. She lay down and spat into the hole. "Coooooooeeeee!" Her voice skittered into the night.

Ben shoved her aside and began cutting the second board.

"We're like burglars," Olive said, climbing back into her camping chair. "Except we're trying to get out, not in."

Ben smiled at her weirdness. The feeling in the cabin had changed now. Hope had blown in. The rain had settled into a steady sprinkle.

"That's cool," Olive said. "I'm a burglar!"

"Now you just have to become a judge and your life will be complete."

"I'd need a wig for that."

Ben heard a noise and stopped sawing. A bird or animal scratching the tin roof.

"This is a secret, okay?" he said. "A proper secret. Like, if they come back, we cannot say *anything* about it . . . or you're dead."

Olive nodded and yawned. It was around nine o'clock, Ben reckoned. She went to bed at eight at home. He wondered what they would do once they had made it through the three boards. Would they really go out into the night by themselves, the only humans in all that inky forest-ness? And what then—tomorrow and the day after?

They're not coming back. The annoyingly honest and fearful part of Ben's mind whispered these words. He hated them now, and hated himself for making them go. Why did he think he could play detective? He slipped with the saw and cut the top of his finger. The pointer, right where he had sliced it on the sharp reed down by the river. Fresh blood spilled from the slit onto the floorboards. He put the finger to his lips and sucked for a few seconds, then pressed down hard on the cut with his thumb, trying to stop the flow. It stung but he knew that he had to keep working. Two boards to get through.

They're not coming back. These words helped him to saw faster and harder. Droplets of blood spat onto the floor. Twin angels of fear and anger drove him on. It was easier now with one floorboard gone. Three-quarters of an hour later he was through another and he started on the third and final board. He wondered if the saw on his knife was getting blunt. He sawed until he forgot about his parents, forgot why he was sawing, and eventually he pulled up the third board.

They were free to leave.

He looked up. Olive had her eyes closed, resting her head against the window frame. He poked her. "Hey, we're through."

"I'm going first," she mumbled, taking her thumb out, sitting up.

Ben was relieved. But he knew he could not let his seven-year-old sister go down through a trapdoor in the night before him. Even a little sister who acted, and maybe was, slightly braver than him.

"I have to," he said.

"Why? Because you're a boy?" she asked, disgusted, shining the flashlight into his eyes.

"No, because I'm five years older than you." Ben was trying to sound convincing, as if he really wanted to go first.

Olive didn't say anything more. *Nuts,* he thought. *She could have at least put up a fight.*

He sat and let his legs dangle into the outside world.

"Maybe we should wait till morning," he said. "There's no point going out now. What are we going to do?"

"We're going out," she croaked. "We've been locked in here forever."

He listened for rain. It had stopped. Just the rushing sound of the river.

"Go on," she said.

The promise of seeing the river by night was enough to move him. He rested his palms on the floor either side of the hole and lowered his legs through the rough-sawn, splintery square. He scratched his hips and bottom through his shorts as he shoved himself downward. Ben wished that he had made the hole slightly wider. Or that he had kept up his exercises at home or not eaten that entire block of chocolate. The soles of his shoes touched corrugated iron and then earth. He smiled.

Ben grabbed the flashlight from Olive and forced the rest of his body down through the hole. He knelt and shuffled the corrugated iron and some bottles aside. He looked out into the forest of pines as Olive's legs appeared through the hole. He heard the gentle rush of the river, the calls of dozens of birds, insects, and frogs. Olive landed heavily and scrambled out from under the cabin.

"What are you waiting for, Fatso?" she said.

"Can you not call me names?" he said. "If I hadn't sawed the hole—"

"Can't you take it?" she said.

Ben wondered where Olive had learned to be such a punk. It wasn't at school. She had always been like this, even before she could speak. Ben trained his flashlight on her. "What if they come back?"

"Don't care. I'm going. Why else did we make the hole?"

Ben crawled out from under the cabin. They would go down to the river. He could think more clearly down there. He would make a decision: stay here and wait for his parents for who knows how long, or, in the morning, take off with Olive up to the main road.

By the time he stood, Olive was already heading downhill. "Wait!" he whispered.

"Why are you whispering?"

Ben wasn't sure. He just felt that he should whisper in a forest late at night. Olive walked boldly into the dark while Ben scanned the ground with the flashlight, thinking every stick was a snake, every shadow a werewolf or zombie.

He ran to catch up with Olive and grabbed her hand, partly for her sake, partly for his. They were halfway down the hill, almost to the fallen tree that he and Dad had hidden behind, when he heard it. At first it didn't sound like a car. But Ben stopped, and Olive stopped, and they listened.

Run, said a voice somewhere deep within him.

THE PLAN

The car screamed down the final steep section of dirt road, not stopping in front of the cabin but continuing out across the clearing. *Why would they park away from the cabin?* Maybe it wasn't his parents' car. But if it wasn't, who could it be? Low rumble. Brakes. Engine cut.

"Hurry!" Olive pushed Ben up through the hole, scratching his sides and hands. Fresh air and river and freedom disappeared.

Car doors opened.

He took Olive's hands, pulling her up into the cabin in a single movement.

"Ow!" she said.

"Shhh!" Ben hissed, switching off the flashlight.

"That hurt," Olive said, sitting on the rim of the hole in the floor.

The sound of low voices moved quickly across the clearing toward the cabin.

"C'mon!" Ben whispered.

She stood up. "I hate them! I wish they'd never come back."

"What if it's not them?" Ben snuck across to the cupboard at the back and looked for the gun, but all he could make out was the shovel. He grabbed the splintery timber handle with two hands. He stood there in the darkness, trembling, Olive clinging to his arm.

"Should we say something?" she whispered.

The chain jangled at the door.

Ben raised the shovel and tiptoed ever so slowly toward the door.

"Should we say something?" Olive asked again.

Ben said nothing.

"Mum?" Olive called.

More jangling.

"Yes," Mum said quietly.

Ben's shoulders dropped. He released a staggered breath. Then he snapped the flashlight back on, lowered the shovel, and moved quickly to the hole, brushing sawdust down into the night. He jammed the three floorboards into place as best he could with the nails getting in the way, then he grabbed the metal handle of the trunk and shoved it back into position.

Someone fiddled with the padlock.

Ben looked to the floor to see if everything was clear. The knife lay there, covered in sawdust. He grabbed it, snapped it shut, and pocketed it just as the door opened.

"Pack the car," Dad said, charging into the cabin. Ben trained the flashlight on him as he went to the table and began shoving things into a bag.

"What?" Ben asked.

"Don't say 'What.' And get that flashlight off me. Anything you want, pack it in the car. Make it light. No heavy stuff. It's got to go in your backpack. We leave in a few hours."

Ben stabbed the flashlight beam at Mum. She stood in the doorway, handbag hanging limply from her shoulder, exhausted, haggard, her cheeks smudged with eye makeup. Ordinarily Ben would have hugged her, seen if she was okay. But not now. Olive stood, arms crossed, back turned in protest.

Dad headed out the door with a bag and a cardboard box.

"Where were you?" Ben asked.

"We've got to go," Mum said.

That was all.

Ben wanted to shout at her but was too shell-shocked to speak. He wished that he and Olive had not turned back. He wished he was still tramping through the darkness to the river, surrounded by *shhhhh* and other night sounds. Forests are supposed to be dark and unknown. Parents are not. He wondered if he would ever again find his mother's *shhhhh* as comforting as he found the sound of that river.

Mum went to Olive, bent down, tried to hug her, but Olive shrugged her off and moved away, arms still folded, back still turned. Ben wished that Mum was as strong as Olive. He went to the door. The car was parked across the clearing under a low tree. Hidden. They had come down the road so quickly and then hidden the car and said that they were leaving. Was someone chasing them? Did they have the passports?

"Why didn't you leave a note?" Ben asked. "You always leave a note. Tell us what's going on."

Mum stared at him. Ben could feel the pressure of all the unspoken truths thickening the air between them. "We just—" she began, and Ben waited, hungry, needing to hear something, anything, but she changed her mind. "Just get your things."

After twenty minutes of packing the car, Mum and Dad ate dinner by flashlight at the table—cold tomato soup from a can and bread. Mum mainly looked at hers and stirred it. Dad watched the window, looking up the hill. Ben sat with them, a brick in his gut: a solid block of unanswered questions, unknown parts of the story. Olive slept, thumb-sucking, her breathing jerky and fitful.

"Where did you go today?" Ben asked.

Dad licked butter off his knife and swallowed bread in lumps.

"We had to arrange some things," Mum said.

"What? Where are we going? Can we go home?"

"No, Ben," Mum said. "Not home."

"We're sorting out a plan," Dad said, not taking his eyes off the window.

"Would you guys mind if we don't go on any more vacations? They kind of suck," Ben said.

Dad eyed him.

"I just want to go home. I miss making my movie. I—"

"Don't use your whiny voice," Mum warned.

Yeah, Ben thought. *Me using my whiny voice is the big problem here. If I just used a normal speaking voice everything would be fine.*

"We'll catch some sleep and leave around two," Dad said.

Ben tried to sit there and be okay with the not-knowing. After all, he was just a kid and they were adults and this was best for him. They knew. They would take care of him. They were his parents. He tried not to say anything, but the words exploded.

"Why do you listen to him?" he asked Mum. "Why don't you stand up for yourself? You would never have left us like that. Why did you?"

Her chin wobbled, she lowered her head.

"That's enough!" Dad said.

Ben had to get out of there, not be near them, or he would tell them how irresponsible they were, tell them that if they ever locked him and Olive up again . . .

He stood, grabbed his backpack, threw his things in, walked out of the cabin.

"Oi!" Dad said, but Ben kept moving. "Back here. Now!"

Ben slowed just outside the cabin door. He had always listened when his father had spoken. Until yesterday he had never even questioned his father to his face, but whatever bond they had was broken now. This "vacation," whatever his parents had done wrong, the lies, reading his notebook. Everything was in pieces. Ben continued across the clearing.

He would sit in the car until they left. He would not go back inside that cabin, ever. He ripped the car door open, jumped in, and slammed it as hard as he could. He slammed it so hard that the glass in the window shattered and fell like a thousand tiny raindrops. They landed in the car, on Ben's lap, on the window frame, on the ground.

Ben stared in disbelief.

He looked back to the cabin, expecting his father to tear across the clearing like a lunatic. But he didn't. The slamming door must have covered the sound of the shattering glass. He opened the door, stood, and brushed glass jewels off his lap onto the silvery sand. The moon had pushed its way through the clouds above. He dusted chunks off the window frame and the car seat and he sat back down, clicking the door closed.

He let the breath fall from him and licked his dry lips.

Did a broken window mean seven years' bad luck? Or was that only mirrors? Either way, Ben felt that his seven years had begun a few days earlier.

Something good will happen. Something good always happens. Tears welled but his eyes swallowed them in gulps. Ben was scared. His parents were scared, so he was scared. Parents were supposed to know the answers. Or to at least pretend they knew.

He was sitting in the back, behind the driver's seat. In the moon-glow he could see the front passenger seat, the gearstick, and half the dashboard. Just above the gearstick, in a groove that looked as though it could hold another stereo, Ben could see a phone. Dad or Mum's new phone.

He looked out the window, back toward the cabin. He could hear raised voices and the dull thunk of footsteps on floorboards but no one was coming across the clearing. The brick in Ben's stomach grew heavy and sharp at the edges. It gave him physical pain, and his tears fell down his cheeks then. He wiped at them and told himself not to be a baby. He didn't need Dad to tell him that anymore.

Ben didn't want to do what he was about to do. If Dad hadn't read his notebook, if they hadn't been locked in the cabin, he would never have done something like this. But these things *had* happened. He leaned through to the front and took the phone from the cavity. He pressed a button and the screen came to life with a picture of his mum in the front seat, looking up into the camera—posing, big sunglasses, one raised brow. Ben glanced back at the cabin again. He swiped the screen, making his mother disappear.

Evidence. Ben wondered if a real detective would do this. Or if it was unethical. He typed in "6688," the same code as her old phone, then hit the "message" button. No messages. He hit the "phone" button. Three dialed numbers. One from 7:15 a.m. today, which meant that they must have left before that time. One from 8:22 a.m. and one at 3:48 p.m. Ben didn't recognize any of them.

Ben turned to the cabin again. They were moving around. No voices now. Ben had come to fear silence almost as much as he feared the arguments.

He pulled the notebook from his backpack, took the pen out, and jotted the dialed phone numbers in tiny writing near the spine on one of the torn middle pages. Ben knew that it was dangerous to use the notebook again, but he hoped that the numbers would not be seen if someone flicked through quickly.

Ben tapped a few other icons but found nothing interesting. There was a selfie of Mum, and one or two shots of Dad driving, silhouetted against the blurred background. That was it.

He clicked on a folder labeled "Web" and discovered two icons. He hit the first. Nothing. He clicked the second, an orange "M" logo, and there were seven open pages. He tapped one, then another, looking for anything even slightly suspicious.

He tapped a page for a news site search on "Ray Silver," and his eyes rested on a picture that made the brick in his belly twist and turn.

Two pictures, actually. And a headline.

APRICOTS

"Apricots?" Mum asked, offering Ben an open can of fruit with a spoon in it.

Ben shook his head.

"Whipped cream?" Dad said.

Ben looked at his father and took the can of whipped cream, spraying some into the middle of a paper plate.

They sat and ate quietly to the sound of Olive sleep-breathing and the wild noises from outside.

"What's wrong with you?" Dad asked.

"Cat got your tongue?" Mum said.

Ben felt as though he had been transported into an alternative universe. How could they be talking about apricots and whipped cream and cats' tongues, knowing what they knew, what Ben now knew?

Mum had come out of the cabin soon after Ben discovered the news article. He had thrown the phone back into the dash compartment and moved quickly to meet her halfway across the clearing, trying to stop her from seeing the smashed window.

"Come back to the cabin. Have some dessert, get some sleep before we go," she had said. So Ben, guilty, mind roaring, floated back to the cabin.

"Are you over your little performance now?" Dad asked, serving himself another helping of whipped cream. "Storming off to the car like a three-year-old."

Ben tasted a small spoonful of whipped cream. It felt thick in his throat. He rested the spoon back on the table.

"It'll work out," Dad said.

"Maybe we'll go somewhere with a pool. And room service," Mum added.

Ben stared at her, the pores of her skin, that terrible haircut. He almost didn't recognize his own mother. It's a weird day when you realize that your parents aren't who you think they are. Ben wondered if there would come a time when he would realize that he, himself, was not who he thought he was, that he was someone totally different. Someone capable of doing what his parents had done.

Bank Error in Your Favor. That's what the news headline had said on Mum's phone. Then the story . . . *bank mistakenly deposited the funds into Silver's account . . . Silver transferred the money to an offshore account . . . the bank has not yet discovered where . . .*

"I'd like to tell Ben where we're going," Mum said.

Dad looked at her, small trickles of whipped cream gathering at the corners of his mouth. "It's a surprise," he said, straight-faced. Something caught his eye, and he tipped his head to the right, looking out the window and up the hill.

"What?" Mum asked, alert.

"Nothing." But Dad continued to look as they waited, holding their breath. "It's nothing," he said finally, turning back to his dessert. He took the last scoop and stood, going over to the ice chest. He searched inside it as Mum and Ben sat quietly, looking at each other.

"Who ate my chocolate?" he asked, looking up at Ben. "Did you?"

Ben nodded. He wasn't scared anymore.

"Why did you do that?"

Ben did not answer.

"You can clean up the dishes, chuck them into that garbage bag," Dad said. "I should be able to trust you." He gave Ben a little whack on the back of the head.

Offshore account . . . Ben remembered what the article had said . . . *Ray and April Silver* . . . *police asking for witnesses who may have seen them.* He had read this before he had thrown the phone back into the empty cavity on the dashboard. *Offshore.* Overseas.

"Let's go," Dad said. "Ben, clean up. Now."

Ben gathered the plates together, and his mind crunched through the contents of the article. One fragment of a line turned over and over in his mind more than any other.

. . . *Seven point two million dollars* . . .

He couldn't get that number out of his head. Seven point two million dollars. The amount they had stolen. *Offshore account*—where the rest of the money must be.

"Seven point two million dollars." He said the words as he threw the paper plates into the bag. Not loud, but loud enough for them to hear.

Mum and Dad stopped what they were doing.

"What'd you just say?"

"I said . . . seven point two million dollars," Ben repeated.

Dad flew across the room and grabbed him by the neck of his T-shirt, pressing him against the rough log wall.

"You're a real little smart aleck," he said into Ben's face, too close to focus.

"Ray!" Mum barked.

"Why did you do it?" Ben asked. "Why didn't you tell us? Are you going to give it back?"

"Shut up," Dad said, stabbing a finger at him. "Don't say another word. No more questions."

Ben wanted to ask another question so bad. He didn't even know what he wanted to ask, but he still wanted to ask it. Dad pressed him harder into the wall. Ben heard the cotton stitching on his T-shirt tear. Dad maintained his grip, staring into Ben's face for the longest time. His watery eyes seemed to swim with a thousand disturbing thoughts.

But Ben said nothing.

"Useless." Dad released his grip and walked out of the cabin, shouting into the night like a beast.

THINK I BETTER RUN

"Everything will be okay. I promise," Mum whispered. She was running her fingers through Ben's hair, tears falling hot and heavy down her cheeks.

Ben was tucked in bed, eyes closed but wide awake, fully clothed. It was after midnight. Dad snored. Olive made sweet thumb-sucking sounds from time to time. Mum sat on the edge of Ben's air mattress. Ben wanted to open his eyes and tell her about the hole that he had sawed, ask her to come with him, but she would stop him. He knew that. There was no way she would let him run alone. Her tears fell on his face when she pressed close.

"It'll be good when we leave here. It was a mistake to come. We'll go someplace better. I promise."

Ben listened.

"Things will be different from now on, but we need to stick together."

Stick together.

"You must trust me, okay?" Mum whispered into the darkness. "It'll be all good."

Trust.

"Why are you doing this?" Ben asked.

She was silent for a long time. Then she said, "I don't know what else to do."

"Yes, you do. Don't listen to him. Listen to yourself."

She cried in short, painful sobs that shook Ben's air mattress. "I don't think I know how."

Ben turned over, away from her. It felt like a terrible thing to do but he had heard enough. His decision was made.

Soon she stopped stroking his hair. She stood awkwardly, stumbling, almost falling on him. She lay down on her own bed.

Someplace better.

Trust me.

It'll be all good.

Ben didn't like it when people said it's "all good." People only said that when things were not good at all.

Seven point two million dollars.

You could do a lot with seven million dollars. You could buy lots of stuff. Maybe they would buy him whatever he wanted, to keep him quiet. *Offshore account.* That's what the article had said. Wherever the offshore account was, that was where they were going, Ben was certain. He didn't want to go anywhere. Only home. Maybe they would live in Switzerland. Or the Cayman Islands. In movies, wasn't that where people hid money that wasn't theirs? . . . *Mistakenly deposited the funds* . . . If the bank put it into their account by accident, even though Mum and Dad transferred it out, wasn't it theirs? Didn't it belong to them now? Wasn't that just bad luck for the bank? Finders keepers. Maybe Ben's parents could keep it. Was Ben a millionaire? Technically, he was. Could life on the run with millions of dollars be good?

Maybe.

Sure.

Yes.

But if your parents were criminals, did that mean that you were more likely to become a criminal too?

What would Sam Gribley do? The kid in the book. Sam Gribley would run into the mountains and live in a hollowed-out tree and survive off the land. Sam Gribley would eat tubers and weird berries and make a fishing hook out of a twig and train a falcon. Ben wanted to do these things too. Even though he didn't know what a tuber was. Sam Gribley would do what was right, Ben was sure of it. Sam Gribley would run.

And that was what Ben would do. He would do what was right. He would run, and he would tell someone what he knew. He didn't want to leave Mum, but she had made this choice, not him. The choice to take the money. And Dad. They chose this.

His decision made him feel sick. His breathing was tight, measured, silent. He waited like this in the darkness, every muscle tensed. Fifteen or twenty minutes passed.

If he was going to get away it needed to be soon. Before Dad woke up and made them get in the car. Dad was a faster runner than him. He had leg length. He could take Ben down like a wolf chasing a rabbit. Eat him alive. Black and crispy on the outside, raw in the middle.

Ben could hear his mother sleep-breathing now, deep and slow. Dad began to snore again. This was his chance. He carefully, quietly, peeled back the sleeping bag. He tried to mold it into a human shape, which might buy him a few precious moments if they woke.

Ben looked over to Olive's bed next to his.

Olive.

He couldn't take her with him. It would be dangerous.

But leaving her behind could be too. Ben's parents were wanted criminals.

She looked so innocent, her face calm and open. Ben felt bad for all the horrible things he had ever done to her. He wished he had always been kind. But he would leave her. He couldn't take care of her. And he could not face telling her the very bad thing that their parents had done. They would have to tell her. Ben stood, and a floorboard creaked. Why had he not noticed that sound in the day?

Pale moonlight rubbed the edge off the darkness. He could see vague shapes of things—the shadow of the workbench, the table, the cupboard at the back, always hanging open. Ben was sure that something was watching him from that cupboard, but there was no time for fear. He looked at the door. The padlock hung from the heavy chain, locking them all inside. Ben would go out through his trapdoor.

He took a step back. Another board creaked, and Mum made a sound. He waited, midstep, one foot in the air, balanced, too scared to lay the foot down. Three minutes on one foot. He felt like one of his own clay stop-motion figures, waiting for someone to take a still frame and move his leg. He wondered if this was the longest that anybody had ever balanced on one leg. Ben felt great compassion and admiration for seagulls. Eventually he dared lower his foot. Silently.

He bent down and lifted the metal chest that covered his hole. It felt heavier in the dark. His right hand squealed with pain from the sawing he had done. His shoulder ached. Ben squeezed his fingers beneath the small chest and lifted one end of it a few inches off the ground, then swung it aside. He put the chest down but the tip of one finger was jammed underneath—his left pinkie. It pinched him so hard he had to let out a quiet, breathy scream, then he grabbed the handle on the side of the chest and lifted, releasing the trapped finger. The trunk banged to the floor.

Mum sat up straight in bed. Ben lay low. His blood stopped flowing.

INTO THE WILD

Ben's body was pressed flat to the cool roughness of the timber boards. He could see the black shape of his mother as she sat up in bed. How would he explain why he was lying next to a hole in the floor?

He waited for her to rock Dad and wake him. Dad would sit up and grab his rabbit gun. Mum would snap the flashlight on, point it at Ben, and see where he had cut the floorboards. They would know that he was trying to escape, that he was going to tell their secret.

Cool air blew up through thin cracks between the boards, tickling his eyes and nose. The floor smelled like old cheese and onions. He lay there, listening, waiting for the end to come.

Why did I do it?

Then, as quickly as she had sat up, Mum lay back down, rustled for a moment, and was still. Soon, she breathed steadily again. Ben matched his own breathing with hers.

A long time passed before he dared sit up. Stillness. But an odd noise from outside. A tinkling, rustling, and a dull *thud*. He listened. Nothing more. He had to get on with this. Could not stop for every sound or movement. He felt around on the floor, his fingertips touching the roughly hacked line of his escape hole.

He stuck his fingernail into the crack and lifted a board. It came up with a squeak and a twist of nails. The next two boards came away silently. He rested them against the wall next to the hole. Night air rushed in, filling his lungs. He breathed in the deep, dark wilderness.

Ben looked over at the bed. Maybe he could hold on a little longer, escape once they were back in civilization. But Ben couldn't deal with not knowing where they were going next or for how long. This was the moment when he could take charge of his own thoughts and actions. Until now, his parents had been the ones in control. But now they were out of control.

Would she go to jail? Or just Dad?

He heard more sounds outside, odd sounds, but he had to ignore them. Had to go. He dropped his backpack into the hole, gently swung his feet down, and lowered his legs. His sneaker soles hit the hard-packed dirt. He pushed the rest of his body through the hole, scraping his sides worse than before. He knelt, and the night washed over him. Trees stood darkly shadowed against the faint glow of moon. Crickets and frogs croaked and buzzed nearby. The river said, *"Shhhhh."* Mosquitoes attacked his arms, and he scratched their bites. He had to get moving.

Ben Silver was free.

He looked up at the hole. It would be so easy to go back. Easier than to go forward. He closed his eyes and wished that everything was going to be okay. He wished that he could rewind time. He wished that they had never come to the cabin. He wished that he was still at home, before the police had knocked on his door and set this in motion. He wished that he was making his movie, and only pretending about zombie thieves and forests and being on the run.

This was it. Clouds must have smothered the moon, because suddenly the night looked darker. The only things he knew out there were the river and his raft. He had already decided that he would use the raft. But what lay beyond, farther downstream? This was stupid. "Better the devil you know." That's what people said. If there were two choices and they were both bad, you should go with the one you knew. *Your own family. Flesh and blood,* said the voice in his mind, the voice he could not control.

There was a jingling sound and a *kshhhh*.

Ben looked to his right, squeezed his bottom lip. He quietly, carefully crawled to the edge of the cabin and looked up toward the clearing. It was dark and still. He watched. Listened. Sticks and leaves crackling underfoot. Something up there. Someone. Ben did not breathe. For a full minute he waited, only his eyes moving, like an owl's.

Kshhhh. A radio. That was the sound. Like his orange and green walkie-talkies at home. Like the one on Dan Toohey's belt.

Then the shape. Behind a tree about a hundred feet from the cabin, at the bottom of the final steep hill on the dirt road. The figure motioned to someone farther up the hill. Then there were two shadows at the base of the forever-tall pine.

Had they seen him? He did not think so.

Were there more of them? He squinted, looking up the dirt road.

What to do. Would he run? Olive. He thought of Olive.

On the corner, up the road, he saw white. The front of a white car.

This decision could change his life. Would he run alone like the zombie thief in his movie? Would he surrender? Or would he listen to the voice at the back of his mind and wake them, warn them?

Flesh and blood.

FLESH AND BLOOD

Ben pulled slowly back from his position and crawled beneath the hole in the floor. His knuckles pressed into the dirt. His eyeballs throbbed in time with his pulse. He felt tears in his eyes, body supercharged with adrenaline. Fight or flight. That's what they called it. Would he fight or fly?

He needed to tell his parents. They should escape too. Through his hole. He would still run but he could not leave them to be caught. No matter what they had done. He needed to help them.

Were the men behind the tree police? Or people after the money? Were they wearing uniforms? He could not see. Hats? He could not remember. Radios? Certainly.

Ben looked up. He reached into the hole. He stood and squeezed the top half of his body into the cabin.

"Psst," he whispered quietly, glancing up at the window, expecting dark shapes to appear.

His parents lay still.

"Pssssssst," he said a little louder.

No response.

One more time, he thought.

"Pssssssssssssssst."

His mother stirred. She sat up.

"Mum," he whispered.

She looked around. "What?"

Too loud, Ben thought.

"Down here."

She turned to him, to the dim, moonlit outline of the top half of his body.

"There are people outside. Police, maybe. You have to come."

The next few seconds happened in a heartbeat. Mum alerted Dad and Olive and they were silently up and out of bed, and Olive's half-asleep body was being passed down through the escape hole to Ben.

"What are we doing?" she grizzled. Ben's instinct was to put his hand over her mouth but he knew it would upset her and she might start screaming. So he simply leaned very close to her ear as Dad dropped the gray sports bag with the black straps through the hole and Mum lowered herself down.

"We must be very, very quiet," Ben told Olive. "It's hide-and-seek. Can you be quiet?"

Olive nodded her head sleepily and sucked her thumb, then she took a sharp breath.

"Where's Bonzo?" she whispered.

Ben panicked. "He's hiding," he whispered, close to her ear. "We have to find him, but we must be so, so quiet. Rabbits have very good hearing."

She nodded a small nod in the darkness. Mum huddled close to Ben now. Dad's legs were through, and he grunted quietly as he pushed his hips and bottom down. The tiny metal studs on his jeans scraped on wood.

Ben heard more noises from up the hill and he passed Olive to Mum and crawled to the edge of the cabin, looking up to the tree where the two figures had stood.

They were no longer there. The white car hood could still be seen up the dirt road and through the trees. But where were the men? At the cabin door? At the window, watching his father escape?

Dad twisted and squirmed to pull his shoulders and arms through the hole.

Finally, all four of them were under the cabin. Their family. Dad handed Bonzo to Olive, and she hugged Dad's arm to thank him.

Ben motioned for his father to join him near the edge of the cabin. He placed his hand on his father's shoulder, whispering very carefully and quietly in his ear.

"I saw two men here." He pointed. "Car up there. They had radios."

Ben could not believe he was helping his parents escape when he should have been turning them in. *Culpam Poena Premit Comes*—the police motto. Ben figured it must be something about honesty, truth, abiding by the law.

Dad scanned the bush. There was a sound from above, at the front door. Dad turned to crawl back beneath the cabin and, as he did, he hit his head on one of the timber beams supporting the floor. This sound set off a chain of events.

An explosive crash came from inside the cabin. A light went on, a moving light. A bright flashlight. Shouting, several voices at once, the kind of raid that Ben had seen on TV.

Dad whispered "Come!" and motioned sharply. He and Mum scurried out from under the far side of the cabin, opposite where Ben had seen the figures behind the tree. Ben watched his parents run off toward a large pine tree farther down the slope. Olive lingered at the edge of the cabin, not knowing whether to run or wait for Ben.

The shouting and loud footsteps continued on the cabin floor above. Within seconds they would see the hole, look down, and find them. Ben's parents had escaped safely and now he would run. Down the hill toward his river, to his raft, and away into the night. But would he take Olive, or leave her? He looked around toward the hole in the floor one final time and he saw something. The gray sports bag. It was lying on the ground directly beneath the hole, the moving, swirling light of the police torches illuminating it occasionally. Dad had left the bag. Ben crabbed backward and picked it up.

"Let's go, Ben!" Olive whispered.

Police above, little sister to his left. Holding a bag filled with what he thought was a million dollars. Would he turn them in, run, or follow his parents who had done the very bad thing? In that brief moment, crouched, panicked, one side of his face lit by flickering beams, the other in darkness, Ben no longer knew if he was a detective or a thief. His dream was to be an officer of the law, but his reality was very, very different.

I'm me, said a voice in his head.

Not now, Ben thought.

I'm me, said the voice again, *but they are me too. My own blood.*

He felt paralyzed. He could just make out the shape of his parents about ninety feet away, behind the tree, motioning for Olive and Ben to follow. But would he? All of these thoughts and actions happened in a matter of seconds but it felt like minutes to Ben. An annoying sister and criminal parents who lied to him, locked him up, showed no remorse.

Run, said another voice.

But they were his family, the only family he had.

I'm me, but they are me too.

"Stop!" said a loud voice as a head appeared through the hole and a sun-bright flashlight beam landed on him. Ben grabbed Olive by the hand, the bag of money in his other hand, and they scrambled out from under the cabin. He put his backpack on, and they started toward Mum and Dad. At that moment a police officer ran down the left side of the cabin, cutting them off from their parents. Without thinking, Ben changed direction, and ran steeply downward. Olive was right behind him. He could barely make out the tree trunks. It was like running blindfolded. He simply had to trust. He felt the trees rather than seeing them.

"Ben. Olive!" Mum's voice, desperate-sounding.

Bang! Doors slamming, and shouting from the cabin. Three, four voices. The other police officers would be running to the door and down the hill after Ben and Olive. The officer who had cut them off from their parents was thudding heavily through the pine forest behind them and off to the left. Ben didn't know if he could see them.

Sam Gribley would have left earlier. He'd be eating turtle soup or making acorn pancakes downstream somewhere. He wouldn't be in this mess. I wish I was in a book, Ben thought. *Things are easier for characters in books. Things turn out okay.* But this did not feel like it was going to turn out okay.

Bad plan, said another voice.

Shut up, he thought.

He tripped on a rock, hit the ground, falling forward. His head hit something hard and there was a bright white flash that stopped everything.

THE FUGITIVE

"Police!"

That word ejected him from the moist night ground, dizzy and hurting. He grabbed the bag and ran again, saying, "Come on! Come on!" and Olive followed, holding his hand. Adrenaline bolted helter-skelter through their bodies, and his forehead ached. The police officer's flashlight beam was still off to the left, but closer now, stumbling down through the trees.

Bad plan, bad plan, bad plan. Those were the words running through Ben's head as he pulled the raft down over mossy boulders and into the darkness toward the river. The rocks were difficult enough in the day and impossible in the black of night.

Just as he felt the front of the raft hit the water, Ben slipped on a rock, banging his tailbone hard. A yelp escaped him, and pain screamed up his spine, but he stood right away. No time to stop, no time for pain. Ben pushed the raft into the river. He looked back up the hill and saw two flashlight beams probing the trees like lightsabers.

His feet sloshed into the shallows and he realized that he had no idea if the rebuilt raft would float with a human on it. He prayed that, this time, it was seaworthy. Ben made a silent vow that if he made it out of this alive he would take swimming lessons. He wondered if prisons had swimming pools.

"Get on!" he whispered, and Olive climbed onto the raft, clutching Bonzo by the ear as she crawled to the front. The raft wobbled side to side.

"Spread your weight. Spread out and hold this." Ben passed her the bag of money. He still wore his backpack. He held the raft steady, pain shooting up from his tailbone, and guided it into the middle of the dark, flowing river. Knee-deep, waist-deep, chest-deep. The water was black ink but for a few patches of moonlight poking through the tips of the tall hoop pines.

The cold numbed the pain in his tailbone. Voices slashed through the darkness. Threats. Where were Mum and Dad? Caught?

The flashlight beams were flying down the incline toward the river now, spraying light through the trees. Ben swam, kicking hard with his legs and holding the front corner of the raft. Olive lay still and flat, the water lapping over her shoulders and legs. He knew that she couldn't swim well either. She hugged Bonzo and the bag of money.

The current took them. Ben wanted to laugh and cry at the same time—laugh with nervousness and fear, cry with the knowledge that he was escaping from his parents, from the police.

The flashlight beams painted moving tree shadows all over the rock wall on the far side of the river. Hulking, sinister shadow puppets. Ben paddled along next to the raft now, trying not to make a sound. The river moved quickly, and Ben concentrated on steering away from the line of rocks jutting into the middle of the river.

He began to feel that maybe they would get away with this, when a shot went off and his body crackled with adrenaline. Ben looked back and saw that one of the flashlight beams was riverside. Were they firing at him and Olive?

He dug in and paddled hard. The dark shapes of rocks and ferns stretched into the center of the river up ahead. He tried frantically to guide the raft toward the opening where the river flowed quickly. He looked back and the flashlight beam was moving down the river's bank toward them. They would either be caught in the ray of the flashlight or stuck on the clump of rocks. Ben paddled, not caring so much about noise now, knowing that his life, both their lives, might depend on getting away.

He felt his body and the raft being sucked toward the waterfall.

"We're going down," he whispered, warning Olive. "Down the drop."

"Okay," Olive said quietly.

The water swept them toward the opening between the boulders and the edge of the river. At the bottom of the small waterfall the water roiled and frothed and the foam glowed white in the moonlight.

"Spread yourself across the raft," he said firmly, and she did.

Ben edged around to the back of the raft, his body still in the water. He knew that they would drop six feet over the fall. He knew that the strength of the raft he had built and sheer luck would decide whether or not they made it. This was an impossible option, but so was going back, giving themselves up, giving their parents up.

They were powered through the gap in the rocks with a gale-force rush, down and over. Ben was airborne, trying to push the back of the raft down as he followed it. He waited for the slap of raft on water, for the raft to explode into a million splinters. He prayed for Olive and he prayed for himself and for the madness of what they were doing. His feet hit the surging broth below. The front of the raft tipped sharply forward and Ben tried to stop it from nose-diving into the river. There was the slap, and he sank beneath the water, losing his grip on the back of the raft.

In and down.

The raft was lost to him, and his entire world was no breath, muffled roar of water, and blackness. Even with his eyes open he could see nothing and he had no idea which way was up and which way down. This was a relief from the fear and dread that waited for him above the surface. Nothing but darkness. Ben felt the weight of his backpack, and, for a moment, he wished to live down there in the netherworld, where nobody and nothing could get him. Except piranha. Ben had always been afraid of piranha. Even in swimming pools.

Soon, fear for Olive and physical inertia pushed him up and out of the water. His face was filled with spray, and he wiped his eyes and searched in the dark roar of the falls and he wanted to call out but he did not. He waited and he paddled as the river shoved him downstream. He saw Olive's head. She was trying to regain stability. Then he saw the raft. It was under her. She was on it. It had not tipped. It had held together. She was holding the bag of money and Bonzo. Ben kicked hard and he laid a hand on a rough branch on the edge of the raft and they drifted quickly down, saying nothing.

The moon raised its head from behind the trees and for a moment he could see the soft glow of the river and banks ahead. To the left was the tall rock wall and, to the right, overhanging trees. Ben paddled for the trees where there was cover from moonlight—shadows, reeds, rocks, darkness. Darkness would be his friend now. His skin felt cold, but the paddling warmed his insides. He took a mouthful of water, mossy and gritty. He spat it out.

They paddled quietly away from the demented roar of the falls and he listened, body tingling. He felt water in his ear. He tipped his head sideways and shook it out.

He looked behind.

Through the trees he could see a flashlight beam scanning the darkness back where they had set off. They paddled on, drifting close to the right-hand bank under the cloak of shadow, listening to the cries and calls of the police officers behind and up the hill.

"Why did the police come?" Olive asked.

Ben ignored her.

There was a corner ahead, feeding around to the right beneath the overhanging trees. *Where do rivers lead?* he wondered. *Do they lead to oceans? Into a lake?* Why had he never learned this? How far would they go and which direction were they traveling?

Sometimes his feet touched the bottom and he pushed off, away from the bank. He could float like this till first light if the river flowed on. It must have been after one o'clock. Five hours till light, Ben thought. His heart rate calmed, and the adrenaline started to evaporate. He pulled his body up onto the raft. The shouting was distant now, but Ben wondered if they were being followed. Surely two kids could not escape the police.

Just then, there were two more shots. One-two. The sound bounced off the tall stone wall.

"What was that?" Olive whispered, grabbing Ben's arm.

Two shots for who? They were too far away to have been for Ben and Olive. So who were they for? They floated back out into the moonlight. No cover from tree shadows.

"Not sure," Ben said. "Maybe it was car doors slamming." He said it to soothe her, to soothe himself. He prayed for his parents. He prayed that what he had done—telling them about the police—had not led to the end of them.

Ben lowered his head. He saw the reflection of the moon and stars in the water. He imagined that he could dive into that deep, dark sky and fall forever. He wished on the bright white moon, on the river, on the darkness, that everything would be okay, that Mum and Dad would be okay, that he and Olive would make it out of this.

In Ben's stories, the good guys always won. But Ben didn't know who the good guys were in this story. Or when it would end.

HOPE

It was the sound of blades that woke him. The rotors.

Chk-chk-chk-chk-chk-chk. That's how they sounded.

Ben tried to open his eyes but the early sun threw daggers and he closed them again. He felt the gentle bobbing beneath him and the sogginess in his shoes and clothes and he remembered. He sat up. His eyes opened, and he saw red. Blood red in the water. He pushed himself up off the raft and got to his feet. He was waist-deep. The sports bag was still on the raft, but he could not see Olive anywhere. He shivered and he called for her, but she did not respond and all he could hear was the *chk-chk-chk-chk.*

"Olive!" he shouted.

Still nothing.

Ben still had his backpack on. He grabbed the heavy sports bag and waded through the red water, leaving the raft in the reeds on the river's edge. He clambered up the steep bank and looked into the river from above, praying that he would not see Olive in there. He didn't know how far they had traveled or how long he had been asleep.

He shielded his eyes and searched the sky. No helicopter. Not yet. But that's what it sounded like.

"Olive!"

No response. He scanned the surrounding bush. It was muddy here. And rough. Not the shady, ferny coolness of the river near the cabin. Harsher. No pines, just gums, eucalypts. Farther down, some giant trees with enormous roots on the riverbank.

"Olive!"

Chk-chk-chk-chk. That sound from the sky. From a low mountain range behind him.

Ben shivered with the cold and began to run.

"Olive, where are you?"

A high-pitched noise came in reply. A bit like a voice, but he couldn't be sure.

"Olive!" He ran and listened but it was hard to hear as the *chk* of the helicopter moved up behind him. He scrambled through the trees, over the hard, stony ground. "Olive!"

Then her voice. "Ben!" He saw her slight figure in a small clearing up ahead, waving both arms. "They're coming to save us."

No, Ben thought. *Not save us.*

The clearing was carpeted in dead yellow grass. He ran to it as the helicopter came over the mountain range behind. He looked back and he could see it now, flickering in and out of the tree branches. The sound was so much louder. Olive was still waving to the sky.

"We're here!" she shouted. "Here we are!"

"No!" Ben screamed, his voice drowned by the cutting sound of the rotors. He was close enough now that he could grab her and try to drag her into the trees, but she would kick and scream and make it impossible. He had to capture her imagination.

"Wave your arms, Turkey Brain," she said.

"Let's pretend we're criminals on the run," Ben said in a loud voice. "Let's pretend . . . that we have to hide from them."

Chk-chk-chk.

"Why?"

"Come on!" Ben said. "Let's hide. Let's make it fun. Let's see if they can find us." He tried to conceal the desperation in his voice, to not sound aggressive in his pleading. She would smell it. "We're bushrangers. Pirate-bushrangers. Captain Thunderbolt and his sister, Olive, captain of the ship. And they're trying to steal our loot."

She was stuck then. He could see it in her eyes. It sounded fun, but why didn't Ben want to be saved?

The chopper seemed to swing right over them. It was high but so loud, and Ben knew that they had been seen, had been found. This meant a whole lot of things that he couldn't think about at that moment.

"All right," she said, disappointed.

Ben grabbed her hand, and they ran. "This way." They ran for the thickest trees, the heaviest cover. *Maybe we can get away,* Ben thought. Maybe they could escape the police for a second time. He knew how crazy it was, how wrong. He knew that he should not be running from the police, that he should be waving his arms too. But if he was rescued he would have to tell the police what he knew. And if his parents were still alive he couldn't give them up. He was running for them, what he thought they would want him to do.

Chk-chk-chk-chk. The chopper was turning back toward them now. Ben ran for the trees with the enormous roots. There was no path. Low shrubs and bristly bushes scratched at his legs as he pulled Olive through. Dragged her.

"Arrrr!" Olive said. "They'll never catch us."

"Arrrrr!" Ben said halfheartedly, and Olive fell. "Whoops!" He pulled her up and continued to drag her.

"Slow down!" she said.

"We can't. They'll catch us and plunder our treasure."

Olive let out a well-practiced cackle, the cackle she used when she was playing pirates on the trampoline after school. But they were not at home anymore. Ben wondered if they would ever see their house again. He could see the thick brown trunk of the giant tree up ahead, the safety of its roots.

The chopper paused and hovered to their right. Ben stopped at the base of the old tree and glanced up. He could see the white nose and dark blue tail with "Police" written diagonally in white. He had seen dozens of pictures of these choppers but never one in the flesh. He was running from the police. He felt as though his dream of becoming a detective had all but slipped away.

The chopper was swallowed by the thick canopy of the tree. Ben and Olive nestled together, their backs against a fat, tall root. Hard green fruit lay around them in the dirt. Vines ran from the ground up to the branches, a tangled mess. The pair breathed hard, shoulders and heads heaving up and down, air filling and deserting them.

Still that sound, the chopper hovering out of sight. So loud. The *chk-chk-chk* was more like a *whoomp* now.

"Pretty fun, huh?" Ben said.

"Are we really playing pirates?" Olive asked.

Ben did not say anything. He was looking up through the branches, searching for their friend and enemy in the sky.

"Then why did you say we were?" she asked.

Ben shrugged. He didn't know why he had said it. How could this be the right thing to do?

Ben squeezed his bottom lip hard, and the shots from last night echoed in his head again. He was pretty sure the first one had been a warning shot. But what about the two shots as the cabin and the police and his parents had faded into the distance?

Whoomp-whoomp-whoomp. It wouldn't be long, Ben thought. The chopper would land. What would he say? Why did they run?

Kids. They were kids. They were scared.

What would the police tell him about his parents, about the shots? He was afraid of what might have happened to them. Maybe that was why he was running.

"I'm hungry," Olive said.

Ben closed his eyes, took a slow breath.

"Maybe they have food," she said. "I don't want to play pirate-bushrangers anymore. Let's tell them we're here. Let's get rescued."

Ben thought about it. She was only seven but she was smart, and Ben often wondered if she knew more than him. *Maybe we should get ourselves rescued,* he thought. *I mean, how will we survive out here alone? Could we make it back to the cabin? Where else would we go?* He looked at the bag. The zip was slightly open. He could see the money, soggy now from the river, a green hundred-dollar bill on top of a pile. The grim-looking man with the mustache stared back at Ben from the bill. Next to him cannons, images of battle. Ben looked up at the chopper, hovering. *We should turn ourselves in,* he thought. *We should.* But then it moved. *Chk-chk-chk* again.

Ben stood, and Olive too. She ran out from under the tree. Ben watched her go but the helicopter moved away quickly. Thirty seconds later, the sound was gone.

And hope too.

STUCK

"What do we do now?"

Ben shrugged. "I don't know."

"Then why did you stop me waving to the police?"

Ben shrugged again. But he knew why. To protect her from whatever happens to kids after their parents go to jail or die. *Not die,* he thought. *The shots were not for them.* His mind wavered.

"What are we going to do?" she insisted.

Ben walked out from beneath the tree, toward the river. He left the bag of saturated money lying on the ground in among the roots. Was that why he had stopped Olive? Was it to protect his parents, his sister, himself? Or was it to protect the money? Maybe. He hoped not. But maybe. It was a lot of money. The police would take it away.

"Which way should we go?" Olive asked.

Ben looked down into the red-stained river. The red was from a plant, he thought. Too much for it to be blood. But still it made him feel sick. He looked upstream, toward the not-knowing place, where he had been at the mercy of his parents. A place he and Olive could not go back to now. He looked downstream into the unknown shadows and shapes created by the trees on the bank. The river twisted into a gnarled tunnel. He turned and looked into the savage sprawl of wilderness behind him and on the other side of the river. A place to become lost.

For the first time in Ben's life, he could choose to do whatever he liked, go wherever he wanted—and he felt stuck.

"I'm hungry," Olive said.

"What do you think we should eat?" Ben asked.

"Do you have any chips?"

Ben looked at her. "No. I don't have any chips."

"Crackers?" she asked.

Ben sat down at the river's edge and hung his feet off the steep, muddy bank. He peeled his wet shoes and socks off. The river was only about twenty feet wide here with dense bush on the far side. Back near the cabin it had been wider. How far downstream had they floated in the night? He had stayed awake for a couple of hours and couldn't remember when he had fallen asleep, but he did know that the river had been running quickly. He let his backpack slide off his shoulders.

The day was starting to warm, and in the sunny patches steam rose from the moist, damp earth around him.

"What have we got?" Ben asked.

"Huh?"

"In your pockets and stuff. What have you got that could help us?" Ben unzipped his backpack as he spoke. He placed his wet video camera on the flat sandstone rock next to him. His knife and soggy notebook and *My Side of the Mountain.*

A random array of pens, pencils, felt-tip pens, and pencil shavings from the zipper part at the front.

Olive laid Bonzo down, waterlogged and pathetic.

"Is that all you've got?" Ben asked.

She stuck her bottom lip out, nodded.

Ben produced a soggy mess covered in plastic wrap from the bottom of his bag. He placed it in the sunshine next to the other things. A long-forgotten sandwich. Not in the traditional sense. It was more like a handful of mushy porridge with bright blue and green spots.

"What is *that*?" Olive asked.

"Sandwich. It's a bit old."

"I am *not* eating that. I would rather die."

He shoved it at her face.

Olive squealed and ran.

Moldy sandwiches were one of Ben's favorite things in the world. He and Gus had a competition running to see who could find the bluest sandwich in the bottom of their bag. This one was a contender. Ben was annoyed that Gus was not there to see it, and part of him, down near his belly, sank. His old life felt as foreign as this place now.

It was the only food they had, and he knew they might have to eat it if they didn't find anything else soon. He pressed it flat and tried to make it square, so that it resembled a sandwich again. Maybe it wouldn't be too bad once it was sun-dried.

"I'm hungry," Olive said again.

"Do you think telling me fifty million times is going to make food magically appear?"

Olive looked hurt. Ben felt bad for snapping. He heard his mother's voice in his mind: *She's only seven. Give her a break.*

"Well," Ben said. "Maybe we should go look for food." He turned to the trees behind him.

Stay where you can hear the river, he thought. *Don't leave the river.*

"Do we have *any* food?" Olive asked. "What about in that bag?"

Ben looked over at the bag of money lying beneath the tree. He laughed. They had so much money. Ben had once heard Mum telling Dad in an argument that "money doesn't buy happiness." He had thought this strange at the time. Of course money could buy happiness. But now he knew.

"There's no food in the bag," Ben said.

"Are there any shops?" Olive asked.

"No," he said. "There aren't any shops."

Ben felt the force of the wild all around them. In the cawing of crows high in a dead tree and the relentless chirping of insects and the silence of the big blue sky. He was not sure if the force was for or against them. But it was there.

"Do you think Aborigines in the olden days ever ran out of food, like us?" Olive asked.

Ben looked around. Yams. He had heard of people eating yams. Maybe he would find a yam.

"Do you know what a yam looks like?" he asked her.

"A man?"

"A yam."

Olive did not respond.

Sugar ants. He had seen a show once where a guy ate sugar ants right out of the palm of his hand. Ben looked at the ground next to him. There were ants but he didn't know which was a sugar ant and which was just a mean, biting ant.

"What about bush food? Do you know anything about that?" Ben asked.

"Is my veggie patch bush food?"

Ben looked at her.

"I grew some really good radishes. Maybe we'll find radishes!" she said.

"Maybe." Ben hated radishes. He opened the copy of *My Side of the Mountain*, gently peeling the wet, stuck-together pages apart, trying not to tear them. Sam Gribley had survived a year in the wilderness by himself.

"He found heaps of food, didn't he?" Ben said. "Berries, acorns, deer. Remember when he ate a deer and used deer fat for his lamp?"

"That was disgusting. We can't eat a deer!"

He wondered if there were even any deer around here. Sam Gribley had been in the Catskill Mountains in New York. Ben wondered if any of the same things grew here. He was pretty sure there would be no raccoons, weasels, or falcons.

"Nothing we ever learned at school can help us here," he said.

"An Aboriginal man came to my school and showed us how to throw a boomerang once."

"That's helpful," Ben said. "Do you have a boomerang?"

"No," she said quietly.

They sat for a few minutes. Cawing and buzzing all around. The flow of the river.

"Sam Gribley is a survivor. You could drop him in the desert or on the moon and he would find something to eat. We have to think like that too."

"Is Sam Gribley real or made-up?" Olive asked.

Ben put his wet shoes back on without socks. "Doesn't matter," he said. He headed for the giant tree, where he had seen the hard green fruit lying on the ground. Olive followed.

He picked up one of the pieces. "Wonder what these are."

"Figs," she said.

He looked at her.

"It's a fig tree," she said, as though he should know.

He flicked open his knife and sliced off a piece of the fruit. He put it into his mouth. It was bitter and crispy. He spat it out, offered the fruit to her. She put her thumb in her mouth, cuddled her dirty stuffed rabbit, and shook her head.

"C'mon. We're going to find food," Ben said. "There must be heaps out here."

FIRST NIGHT

Imagining that your parents were dead was not a nice feeling, Ben found. Particularly when it was dark and mosquitoes were biting and you were sitting on the ground against a tree and you had no fire and your belly was empty and your little sister Olive had been crying and angry at you and you were angry at yourself.

Life had always seemed hard at home. He had to walk to school and he only got to order lunch once a week and he had to wash the dishes sometimes and put the garbage out and feed the dog every day and shower and remember to brush his teeth. And he had to eat potatoes for dinner even though he didn't like potatoes, except when they were in chip form.

But then, at the cabin, things had seemed harder, with the not-knowing and Dad being more nervous and angry than ever and Ben trying to find out why there was a bag full of money hidden in the roof. Then Mum and Dad locked them in and the police came late at night and they had to escape on the raft.

But now, lying here in the pitch-dark on the damp ground and feeling the deepest fear he had ever felt, he would have done anything to be at home or at the cabin. The cold swept up from the river, blowing through him, eating his muscles, clutching his bones.

He listened. The *shhhhh* of the river calmed him a bit, but he was not listening for the river now. He was listening for the sounds beyond it, and he had never heard anything that scared him so much. It was as though the noises were on his skin and in his ears. *Screek*s and *craaaark*s and *yowl*s from wild things all around.

They had wandered for hours in the day and not found anything that Ben would call food. He had picked grasses, peeled bark, and crushed leaves in his fingers—searching and smelling and feeling for things to eat. Not even good things. Just things. He had thought about eating insects and, in the afternoon, he had eyed off the blue-spotted sandwich, but none of it was right.

They had argued all day about whether to walk upstream or downstream. Ben had laid piles of wet hundred-dollar bills, about a quarter of the money, out in the afternoon sun and dried it. He half hoped that the police helicopter would return. In the end, they had stayed put, and as the sun went down they had each filled up on a bellyful of reddish river water and an unripe fig before snuggling into their tree root home. Ben's stomach was not fooled.

Now darkness had folded in on them. Ben desperately needed to go to the toilet but he would wait till morning. He had never even been camping before. He imagined the luxury of having a tent, fire, a flashlight, a sleeping bag, food.

He had nothing. Just him, wilderness, Olive, fear. Fear was his fire, keeping him alert and alive. Growing up in a house in the suburbs, right next to a highway, had not prepared him for this. Playing thousands of hours of video games, watching hundreds of movies, playing soccer, helping out in the wrecking yard, watching game shows with Nan—none of it was useful to him now. Someone had pressed "reset" on his life. He had no pantry, no fridge, no shops, no cars, no lights, no bed, no blankets, no roof.

He sat up straight, back against the tree. His bottom was wet and cold. He had large leaves beneath him, but they didn't help. He was gripping a short, thick, heavy branch that he would use as a club if he had to.

"I'll go on watch first," he had said to Olive. But he knew that he would be on watch second too. He would stay up all night. Someone had to protect them from animals and insects and strangers and ghosts and police lurking in that fine, silvery moonlight.

Ben had a plan. If anything came for them, he would wake Olive and they would climb the tree. He had worked out the quickest route to the top. Olive was a good tree climber so she would be okay.

He was glad he wasn't out there alone. As the hours passed he watched the moon crawl slowly across the sky, in and out of the branches of the tree above. Each minute felt like forever. When his head drooped to his chest he pinched and even slapped himself. He focused on the moon. He thought about

Pop. When Ben was little he would sit on Nan's back stoop and they would look up at the moon and she would tell him that Pop was up there.

"In the moon?" Ben would ask.

"Yep," she'd say. "Looking down on you. He loved you *so* much."

He hoped that Pop was looking down on him now. That someone, somewhere, was watching over him. And even though Pop had not met Olive before he died, Ben hoped that he would watch over her too.

He needed a plan.

Something to tell Olive.

To make her think he knew what they should do.

To look like they were in control. Not out.

What are we going to do? she would say in the morning.

And he would say . . .

Nothing. He would say nothing.

Icy bottom. Freezing fingers. Cold nose. Aching body.

Plan. Why are we running?

He could not remember.

Running because . . . Mum and Dad did the wrong thing. Because of the money. Because of the police. Because the policeman had cut them off, forced them to run downhill to the raft. Then the gunshots. Dead? Maybe. Sometimes he felt certain the shots were for Mum and Dad. Other times he was sure they were okay.

They could run into the wilderness. Go back to the cabin. Try to make it home to Nan. Or tell the police, hand themselves in.

These were Ben's final thoughts before sleep took him. He did not wake until he heard the footsteps. They were in his dream at first. A man's feet, in boots, close and staggering through undergrowth. Then vines clutching the man's legs, tendrils curling around him, trying to stop him. The man breaking the vines.

But when Ben woke he still heard the steps. They were close. He stood, raising the stick. He wanted to wake Olive, but he was struck silent by the footsteps.

Ben was sure he was about to die. That this person did not mean good things for him. He ruled out police officers. They don't work alone, and Ben was sure it was just one person. Was it a person? The heaviness of the steps sounded like a man or some large animal. His father? Maybe Dad had come downstream in search of them? Should he say something?

Closer now.

Ben pressed himself back into the roots of the tree and squeezed his club tight, ready to beat whoever or whatever it was over the head, ready to protect Olive. Death could not be worse than this. At home he was scared by his parents arguing after he went to bed, hoping that Dad would not leave. But that did not compare to this feeling now.

Slow steps. Close. Steady. Rustling in between. Dragging. Was it dragging something? Ben strained to see through the black, black night. Too late to wake Olive. Too late to climb the tree. He could not control this. It was not a stop-motion movie.

TANGLED

"We shouldn't be doing this," Olive said.

Ben slipped, one foot skidding into the cold river. He pulled himself up onto the boulder. He had his school backpack on and $982,300 in the bag in his hand. He had counted the money, some of it sun-dried and crispy, at first light. Olive had helped. Ben had decided to tell her everything. She had flipped out, could not believe that Mum would do this. Then she started planning what she would do with the money.

"We should be going downstream," she said.

"Upstream," Ben said.

"Down."

"Up," Ben said. "Back to the cabin. Back to Nan's. She'll know what to do."

They used the boulders at the edge of the river as their path, leaping from one to the next.

"We shouldn't have left the raft," Olive said.

"Feel free to drag it up the river if you like."

Ben had not slept after the thing went by in the night. He doubted he would ever sleep again. Not out here. He still didn't know who or what it was or if, in that soup of darkness, dream, and fear, he had imagined it. In his next life, Ben planned to be brave.

"The only thing we have to fear is fear itself."

That line came to him. Who had said that? History teacher. Mr. Stone. Silver glasses, wild gray eyebrows.

"The only thing we have to fear is fear itself."

Was that true? He wanted to believe it, but he wondered if the person who had said it originally had ever been stuck in the wild with snakes and insects and bodies dragging by after midnight.

They had to get back before dark.

"We'll get there by dusk," he told Olive as they trudged uphill.

"And what if the police are still there, Mister Smartypants?" Olive asked. She was just ahead of him.

"Watch out for the mossy rocks."

"What if?" she asked again.

"We'll be careful."

What if Mum and Dad are dead? he wondered. He had not shared his fear with her.

"I hate Mum and Dad."

"Don't say that."

"Well, I do. They wrecked everything."

"They're still our parents."

Later, when the rocks became steeper and slipperier, they were forced to make a path through thick undergrowth beside the river. Scratchy lantana bushes with tiny pink, white, and yellow flowers grew everywhere. Green-leaved vines twisted through it. Tall palm trees soared upward, searching for light through the canopy.

Upstream.

They had been a day and a half without food. But they would eat tonight. They would make it to the cabin and they would find food there.

"I can't go anymore," Olive said eventually. She stopped and dabbed at the cuts and grazes on her arm. She started to cry. Ben felt like crying too, but he could not. He was the father here, and Dad had assured him that real men don't cry.

"Don't be a baby," he snapped, pushing on through thick, bristly vines and ferns, blazing a trail. "I'll have to leave you here." He felt bad for being so harsh but unless he was tough on himself, tough on Olive, they would not make it back to the cabin before dark.

Listen for the river, he kept saying to himself. Sometimes it was easier to veer away from the river, but he could not leave it behind.

"I'm hungry," Olive moaned, scrambling to catch up. "I want to buy something. We could eat anything in the whole wide world with all that money."

Ben was bone-hungry. Blood-and-bone-hungry. Mum always told him to eat less, exercise more. "You don't want kids teasing you for being fat," she would say when he asked for a sundae at the drive-thru. Mum thought that standing out or being teased was the worst thing in the world. Now he was eating less. Eating nothing. He wondered if she would be proud.

"Do you like Mars Bars or Milky Ways better?" Olive asked.

"I don't know," Ben said. "Don't talk about food."

"Which one?"

"I don't know. Mars."

"I like Milky Ways," she said. "Dogs or cats?"

"I've never eaten either."

Olive laughed. "For a *pet*!"

Ben sighed loudly. "Whatever. Cats."

"What about Golden?" she asked. "I like dogs. Lego or TV?"

"Be quiet," Ben said.

"I like Lego," she said. "You can do heaps more than just watch it. Do you like James or Gus better?"

"Neither. I like them both. I miss those guys. I even miss school."

They walked on, absorbed in the bubbling and stirring of the river, the sunlight in dappled patches all around, always moving forward.

"Do you think Uncle Chris knew?" Ben asked. He had been thinking about this a lot.

Olive pulled her thumb out of her mouth. "He gave Dad the bag of money. And that dumb car."

"Dad always said Uncle Chris was dodgy."

"And now Dad's dodgy too," she said.

Ben looked down at the bag of money. He had taken the money and run with it. What did that say about him?

TEMPEST

A camera flash. That's how it looked at first. A bright flash a long way off. But then the wind came too, and he sat up, looking into the tall trees around him. The clouds moved quickly against the dead black sky, all lit up for a moment and then gone again. The lightning was mainly upstream. Olive had worked out that upstream was west, over the mountains. Then came the rumble, and the wind answered it, flurrying around him and whistling ice into his bones.

He looked down at Olive who was lit in fits by the flickering white light. She rubbed her nose in a tired way and cuddled into herself for warmth, then jammed her thumb back into her mouth. Ben wished that he was a seven-year-old thumb-sucker lying by a river, eyes closed, three-quarters asleep, not knowing.

Rush of water, dark of night, wink of lightning, ominous roar, tremble of body, whirling wind. And fear. Terrible fear.

Choices.

Ben had to believe he had choices even now, when it seemed he had none. His mind was foggy. How could he have been so stupid not to build a shelter when it was light? They had walked and walked till it was too late and the darkness had rushed to cover the sky. It had rained two nights since they had left home. The night they had been locked in the cabin and back in the motel, Rest Haven. Flickering fluorescent lights and bedbugs. Ben would have done anything to be lying on those bedbug-ridden couch cushions now.

The first drop of rain landed on his scalp, and it was cold. His arms felt the big, biting splats, and soon he settled down into a deep shiver. It shook low and heavy through his bones like a train through a mountain tunnel. Hips, knees, ankles, wrists, elbows, shoulders, toes, fingers. That's where it bit worst.

"Shelter," he whispered. He needed to find some but he couldn't leave Olive here by the river. What shelter would he find? A cave? Not likely. And the fig trees were a long way downstream now. At the edge of the river here there were just tall, naked palm trees and lantana.

The sky snarled and the wind picked up and the rain forest all around hissed and warned him not to enter. But he would. Had to. He stood, shouldered his backpack, and picked up Olive and Bonzo and the bag of money. Lightning lit Bonzo's right eye, and it reminded Ben of the rabbit on the chopping stump.

Ben stepped to another rock, heading up the bank, and the bag fell away from him. One of the handles tore and, in the flickering light, he saw four wads of cash fall through the broken zip. He panicked, even though he could not care less about the money now.

He put Olive down and bumped her head on a rock and still she did not wake. He reached down and grabbed at one of the piles of cash on the rock and it slipped into a crack. It fell into the water and floated off down the river in the flashing white light. Fifty thousand dollars, he thought. It meant nothing. It could have been fifty cents.

He stuffed three piles of money back into the bag and left it on the riverbank for the moment as the rain began to teem. He picked Olive up. The rain roared in his ears and thunder made the ground quake beneath his feet as he ran. He was so cold. Bushes slashed at him. He went on like this for five minutes.

The dark outline of a giant tree, not a fig, loomed ahead, rising like a mushroom cloud in a blast of white lightning. Olive had pointed one of these trees out in the day as they forced their way upstream. He rested her against the trunk, still asleep. He ran out through the rain. He gathered fern fronds and anything soft that he could find and he ran back beneath the tree and made a bed for Olive. He laid her on it.

Rain still pelted through the tree canopy, so he gathered branches from the ground around them. The pain of exhaustion sawed through him. Ben tried to erect something like a tepee over Olive. He put four, seven, ten sticks up into a cone shape as she slept. He used his knife to cut fern fronds and wove them through the sticks, trying to protect her from the wind.

The money flickered into his mind, but, still, he left it, beside the river. For all he cared it could fall in and float away. He collapsed under the tree, ripped his backpack off, shivering, and the rain streamed down his face.

Things will get better, he thought. *This is as bad as it gets.* As sleep gripped him, he had the feeling of melting down into the earth. There was no difference between him and the ground and the trees and the rain and the river. All one.

THE END

Scratched, bruised, tired, dehydrated, vomiting. That was how Ben found himself as the talons of first light scraped his eyelids. Lying on a flat rock on the edge of the fast-moving river, using the bag of money as a pillow. Water taking leave of his stomach.

Mosquitoes had woken him an hour before dawn. With the storm gone, he had been drawn to the river. He'd vomited and fallen asleep on the rock, too delirious to worry about Olive back at the tree.

"You okay, Thunderbolt?" said a croaky voice behind him.

"Yep," Ben said, his throat acid.

"Why did you move me?"

"Storm."

"I was sick in the night too," she said.

Ben felt it rise up in him again. He leaned over the edge of the rock and dry-retched, body tingling, trying to force whatever it was out of him. Nothing would come.

Olive squatted and rested a hand on his back. "Are we going to die?"

He splashed his face and looked upstream through the wall of water dripping from his brow. Exhausted, light-headed, still cold.

"No," he said. "We're not going to die. But we need to eat. It's been two days." Ben looked at her. She had thick, dark rings under her eyes. Her nose was snotty. She was skinny and dirty and weak-looking. It was Ben's fault.

That morning they ate whatever they could find. They couldn't hold out any longer. They foraged and gathered. They worked out which things looked less likely to kill them—grass, flowers, plant bulbs—and they used Ben's knife to harvest the food. Olive nibbled leaves, and Ben found a fat white witchetty grub buried in the soil beneath a rotting log. The feel of it in his mouth made him grimace, but the flavor was nutty and good. He dug deeper into the soil and found two more. They leaked brown water over his fingers, but he ate them quickly, crunching through the skin to the soft, gooey stuff inside. Olive would not try them. She ate the crisp, juicy tips of fern fronds instead, nibbling at them like a pink-eyed rabbit, holding her nose to block the taste. "This is hor-ri-ble."

They heard a helicopter in the distance and Ben willed it toward them, but they could not see it through the trees and, after a few minutes, the sound deserted them. The disappointment kicked him in the ribs.

They made slow progress, slower as the morning wore on. They argued, and Olive refused to walk. She complained of stomach pains. It was hard to know if it was the river water or the strange foods. Ben carried the money tucked under his arm now that the strap had broken. It was awkward and heavy and it blistered his side.

The money.

Ben had always figured rich people were the very best kind. Lucky and smart and good-looking and happy.

"He's got six properties!" Dad would say about some guy he had met at a barbecue. "He says the secret is to never sell one before you buy the next. And never get a loan. The banks are the enemy."

"Right," Mum would say in the car on the way home. "And how are we going to do that?"

"Leave it to me," Dad would say.

"Okay."

Ben believed Dad when he said things like that, even if Mum did not. He knew that Dad would come through in the end. Sometimes Dad would take Ben aside and tell him how rich they were going to be and how big his new business venture was and that a guy he knew at the pub had made heaps on it. "It's a good product," he would say. "You have to believe in the product if you want others to believe in it."

"Definitely," Ben would say in a really interested way that made them both feel good. This was before Dad had bought the wreckers. When he was still hopeful.

One time Dad was selling a cleaning product that could shine silver better than any other product in the whole world. He showed Ben by shining a 1992 ten-cent piece till it looked new. Ben could not believe how good it was and he knew that people were going to buy crates of it. Who wouldn't want coins that shiny?

But they didn't.

"People are idiots," Dad told him.

Now Ben had $932,300. Fifty thousand had washed away. But he did not feel smart or lucky or good-looking or happy like the rich people in his imagination.

That afternoon Olive went downhill fast. Diarrhea at first, then Ben noticed a spotty rash on her arms and face. She vomited and cried and eventually she could not walk anymore. Ben carried her on his back with his backpack, his legs weak and buckling, the bag of money grating against the weeping blister on his side.

At some stage Ben noticed that he had stopped speaking to himself. His mind, usually roaring with thoughts and ideas, flatlined, leaving just a deep, grim determination to make it to the cabin. But soon the sun hid behind the hills and the forest turned to shade. Olive did not speak or move now, a deadweight on his back. Just two little koala claws clutching his shoulders. And Bonzo the rabbit hanging limply from her fist. Even Bonzo did not look hopeful.

Ben stopped every ten minutes or so to check on her, to search for her pulse, open her eyelids, to speak to her. He felt that awful brick-in-the-belly fear. Twilight fell into night and he stopped and shook her gently and he said her name and spoke to her as though the words would heal her somehow. But they did not, and she would not take river water or any of the roots or crispy fern frond tips.

"Olive, please wake up," he said into the murky dark.

He feared that she was as good as dead if he didn't get her back to the cabin or to some kind of help, and he blamed himself for all of it. He called out to the forest, screamed for help that night for nearly an hour, but his voice fell on nothing and no one. There were only the animals, and he was sure they would help if they could. But they could not.

THE WRECKERS

Gray light crawled into the sky, and Ben came to from a deep, eyes-wide-open doze. He looked down at Olive, who was lying across his lap, limp.

"Olive?" he said.

He shook her gently.

"Olive, it's day."

She didn't seem to care. He watched her chest but he couldn't see it moving in the gloom. He put his fingers to her neck and found no pulse. Dread shot through him even though he knew that he often had trouble finding his own pulse—and he was alive. He pressed his fingers under the other side of her jaw, and at last he felt the deep throb of her life against his skin and he had never been more thankful for anything.

He looked around.

Today, he thought, and as the word came to him through the gray of early morning, he saw the silhouette of a pine tree.

Ben had not seen a pine tree in days.

He stepped carefully from boulder to boulder, sloshed into the river, Olive on his back with his knapsack. On the far side of the river, trees gave way to the beginning of the rock wall that he knew from his days at the cabin. He laughed. It was an unhinged laughter that he had not heard from himself before.

"This is it!" he said to Olive. Her cold, grubby cheek was pressed flat to his shoulder blade. She did not respond. "This is it."

Ben stumbled for ten minutes in the shallows as the river wandered deeper into the pine forest. His knees cried in pain. He could hear the waterfall. It was drawing him upstream, like a fish on a line. Soon he saw a rough dirt path beside the river, and he made good time then.

Ben thought of the police helicopter and he wished he had not been so stupid, had not hidden from the police and almost killed his sister. As he climbed the hill, past where Dad had shot the rabbit, he called out, "Hello!"

Birds.

"Hello!" he screamed.

He could feel the weight of the money rubbing at the raw place under his arm. He would hand it over if the police were there. He would tell them everything. He made it into the clearing and he looked around and he almost cried.

The police were not there and his parents were not there and the car was gone and the door of the cabin hung open. He dropped the money, lurched and swayed to the door, broken from the climb, Olive still on his back. It was mostly empty inside, cleared out apart from the furniture. The food on the shelf, the ice chest—all gone. How long had it been since he was here? Three days, he was pretty sure.

He laid Olive on the workbench, the bench that he had been standing on when he discovered the bag of money in the roof. He cried then. He didn't care what Dad would say anymore. He cried so hard for his little sister and for his maybe-dead parents and for himself and for the whole state of the world. He cried because he knew that he and Olive would get out of this alive and because, from here on, life would have no certainty.

Outside, the birds heard him cry and the frogs stopped and listened and the trees stood darkly against the morning sky.

The river flowed on.

Mangled steel. That's what he dreamed of as he lay on his side on the cold timber floor that night. The wrecking yard. Piles of mashed metal. Carnage. Other people's problems. When someone took their eye off the road for a moment to adjust the volume and got T-boned by a semitrailer or they ran a red light and mistimed it and hit a motorbike, that's where Dad came in. Other people's bad luck: he fed off it. He would race out there in the tow truck, pick up the car, come back, hack it up, sell it off, or crush it. He was a wrecker. That's what he did. He wrecked stuff. Mum helped. Cars, trucks, motorbikes, Ben's life, their family. Themselves. They wrecked themselves and they left Ben and Olive to deal with the mess.

And now where were they?

His eyes flicked open. It was dark. They had slept the entire day away. Ben hadn't had the energy to get Olive up to the main road. Not yet.

Olive lay next to him, sleeping on the torn canvas camp bed against the wall. He sat up and looked at her still, pale face and listened to her breathing.

Earlier in the day, they had eaten from a plastic garbage bag in the corner of the cabin, food thrown out on that final night. Food from the garbage was like a royal feast when you hadn't eaten real food in days. A third of a can of apricots, the can of whipped cream, and an ancient can of baked beans in the back of the scary cupboard at the rear of the cabin. But the cupboard wasn't scary anymore. He was no longer afraid of the dark or of night noises.

He had given Olive small sips of water from an almost full bottle he'd pulled out of the garbage bag. She took it in drops. He fed her beans. She'd had two mouthfuls before falling into a deep sleep, breathing short, shallow breaths.

Ben had to think. The decisions he was about to make were important. No more bad choices. It was black-dark, and he did not know what the time was. His body ached with cold. He grabbed his backpack, stood, went to the table. Moonlight leaked from the window onto the work surface. He sat on the table, legs crossed, and pulled out his damp notebook and pencil. He wrote down what he thought might happen once they made it back to Nan's:

Mum and Dad alive. Head out on the run again.
Mum and Dad alive. In jail. Live with Nan or sent
somewhere else.
Mum and Dad dead. Live with Nan.
Mum and Dad dead. Get sent somewhere else.

Ben read his list. He had never liked multiple-choice tests. His eyes circled back to the words "Mum and Dad dead." He could not believe he had written them.

"Not dead," he said to himself. "Parents don't just die."

But parents don't just steal millions of dollars either. Only they do.

Ben needed to be careful. Needed to make a good choice. Would he become a wrecker too? His parents were criminals, so he must be more likely to become one. Like father, like son. Did he have a choice or was it written in his DNA?

He turned to the bag of money, which was in the corner nearest the door. Broken zip, one handle snapped. Damaged and pathetic. An idea occurred to him. Something he would not write down. Could never write down or tell anyone except, one day, Olive. He would keep it locked in the vault of his own thoughts where no one could steal it. He sat there for a very long time watching the money, turning the idea over in his mind, twisting himself inside out.

Could he do it? Was it right? Did "right" matter anymore?

Eventually he stood from the table. He walked across the room, bare feet on floorboards, to the yawning cupboard at the back. He reached into the blackness of it and he took out a shovel.

THE ROAD

Ben held his arm out straight and stuck his thumb up the way he had seen it done in old movies. He had a feeling that people didn't use the thumb anymore. Where Ben came from people did not hitchhike.

Olive lay at his feet in the sandstone gravel of the roadside, her head on his bare, blistered foot, eyes closed, saying nothing. That was the thing that worried him most: Olive not speaking.

He listened for the river. As they had walked up the steep dirt road from the cabin he had listened for it till the last. Then the umbilical cord had been cut and the sound was gone. Just Ben and Olive. Now he thought he heard it again, like the distant sound of the ocean in a shell. But the sound was a car. It appeared around the big bend a couple of hundred yards up the road. A small yellow hatchback filled with passengers. As it passed, someone screamed at them from the window.

"Have some water," Ben said, bending down to offer Olive the dregs of the bottle he had found in the cabin.

She did not respond.

They waited a long time, maybe twenty-five minutes, for the sound of another engine. But what turned the bend was a motorcycle, not a car, and it sped past them down the hill and away.

A week earlier Ben would have been beaten by this, would have been angry and frustrated and scared. He would have thought that the world was out to get him, but now he did not expect so much. Things could not rattle him so easily. Maybe not even death. He would not get carried away with things, good or bad.

After ten minutes another engine, louder, lower. A truck, Ben was sure. In his clouded, tired mind he calculated that there might only be two seats in a truck and some part of him gave up hope, but he looked down at Olive and he knew that he had to stop the truck.

It rounded the bend, a semitrailer with a green cab and dozens of long logs on the back. Ben waved his arms wildly.

"Help!" Ben called. "Stop!"

Olive was startled by the shouting and tried to stand but she faltered and dropped to her knees. Ben wanted to comfort her but he knew that his job was to get them home, to get them to Nan's. The truck moved past them and there was no way the driver could not have seen them. Ben watched the back of the truck recede, but still anger did not rise up in him.

He coughed heavily. His lungs ached.

Red lights and a deep groan farther on, before the steep hill that led to another faraway bend. The truck's red brake lights. Maybe just slowing for the hill, Ben figured, but then it pulled to the side, rocks kicking up, blinker on.

"This is us." Even as he said the words, Ben did not believe them.

Olive didn't seem to hear him. She was lying down again so he scooped her off the ground, balancing her across his arms as he walked-ran toward the truck, which was still slowing, half-on, half-off the road. Every molecule of energy left in his starving, exhausted, bleeding body went into that run. He reached the truck as it finally pulled up with a *ssss* and a crunch of tires on gravel. He ran alongside the truck, and the driver watched him in the dirty passenger-side mirror. The door popped open and swung over Ben's head. The driver—neatly shaven, brown shirt, sunglasses, kind of old-fashioned-looking—met them with a smile. He had good teeth, Ben noticed. He would have thought that truck drivers didn't brush their teeth very often, but this one did.

"Thank you," Ben said. He prayed that the driver didn't recognize them, that he and Olive had not been in the news too.

The driver looked down at them, at their dirty, ragged clothes. "You lost?"

"Sort of," Ben said.

DEAD OR ALIVE

He listened. With every ring he clutched the phone more tightly. Why wasn't she home? Nan never went out.

The pay phone was in a timber bus shelter crammed with backpackers sitting on their luggage. Cars crawled by on Kings Bay's main street. Olive sat on the ground, eating an electrolyte freezer pop from the pharmacy, listless.

The truck driver had let them out at the hospital on the edge of town, had told them that Olive needed to see a doctor, had offered to come in, but Ben said, "No." Ben and Olive had gone inside, then Ben waited till the truck was out of sight and walked into town, Olive on his back. He couldn't take her for medical help because he would have to give their names. They might be recognized. Ben had three crisp hundred-dollar bills in his pocket, taken from the gray sports bag, and he bought new clothes for each of them and a bunch of medicines from the pharmacy. He received some curious looks when he handed over the cash to pay but no one questioned him. Dad was always telling Ben, "Money talks." Ben figured this is what he meant. He tried to heal Olive, and she had eaten. Not much, but she had.

The phone continued to ring. He wondered if the phone might be tapped, if he was putting Nan in danger. He remembered, from a movie, that you could tell if a phone was tapped: you'd hear a small beep or click a few seconds after the call began, when the recording started. But was that a really old movie? He couldn't remember.

Finally, after almost a minute, "Hello?"

"Nan. It's Ben."

He did not hear a click or a beep, but he still didn't say much. He did not tell her everything. Just that they were alive, that they would see her soon.

And then the question that he was most afraid to ask: "Have you seen Mum and Dad?"

She paused for a long time before she answered.

At the bus station Ben bought two tickets for the 4:30 p.m. bus out of a machine. A lady with short gray hair regarded him suspiciously from behind the information counter. Ben lowered his head and tried to keep Olive out of sight, hidden by the machine. Ben wondered if the lady had recognized them, if their story had been on the news. How many people knew they were missing? And which was worse—the thought of everyone knowing, or no one?

The journey down the coast was slow. Olive fell asleep the moment they sat in their stained, threadbare seats, second row from the front. He watched her carefully, wondering if he had done the right thing by not taking her to the doctor.

"Going home," he said quietly. She sucked her thumb, cuddled Bonzo.

Ben fought to stay awake, sipping a steaming cup of milky coffee he had bought from a machine outside the station. He missed the sound of the river, missed the feel of it, even though he was thankful to be somewhere warm and comfortable. He closed his eyes and tried to hear that *shhhhh* in the white-noise whir of tires on wet road.

"Click flutter, flutter click," said a woman behind them, over and over again, her voice low and unnerving. Ben peered through the gap between the seats. She had white-blond hair, messy lipstick. She bit her nails loudly—*click tick tick*—repeating the words "click flutter, flutter click" again and again.

Across the aisle was a small, straight-backed woman wearing fluorescent yellow jeans and zebra-print boots. Her feet did not touch the floor of the bus. Behind her, leaning against the window, was a man with a skeletal face and wild green eyes that shone bright in the passing headlights. He turned to Ben and asked him something but Ben could not hear the words. Ben smiled, tried not to look scared, and turned away.

When the coffee had gone through him, he went to the bathroom at the back of the bus. He took Olive with him, guiding her unsteadily up the aisle.

There were about twenty passengers. Most of them looked broken in some way, Ben thought. They wore the scars of hard lives in their faces and in the way they sat. When Ben was little, he hadn't known that people could become broken. Toys and plates and windows, he knew, but not people. Now he knew they could. Not just hairline fractures but compound breaks, where the bone pushes through the skin. Like when Olive broke her arm when she was four. Ben wondered if he would become broken like that someday.

Hours later, when everyone else on the bus was asleep, Ben drifted into an unsettled nap. He woke regularly to check on Olive, expecting to be leaning against the roots of a fig tree or lying on a rock or flat against cabin floorboards.

Olive woke around midnight.

"Can I have some water?"

Ben gave her some. She lifted her head from his shoulder and drank slowly.

"I'm hungry."

He had not heard her say that in a couple of days. He reached for his backpack, jammed with food. She nibbled a rice cracker for a few minutes, then asked, "Where's the bag? The bag of money?"

Ben's heart thumped.

HIDE-AND-SEEK

He bolted down the alley, battered backpack on his front, Olive on his back. Morning light. Litter everywhere. Fences to the right and a wide concrete drain to the left. He slowed, looked both ways, took a deep breath, and shoved through Nan's squealing back gate into the long grass of her yard. Golden barked angrily and ran at them.

"Let me down," Olive said, and Golden whined in a happy way. Ben let Olive down gently. She knelt. Golden licked her face, then ran across the yard like a maniac, doing circuits around the clothesline, past the tumbledown chicken coop and the old white car wreck that Dad had brought home when he was seventeen.

"Shh! Shhhhhh!" Ben said to Golden, trying to calm her. He pushed the gate shut and walked up to the house. Light blue peeling paint. He climbed onto the timber back veranda, avoiding the rotten stairs. He knocked quietly and heard the familiar squeak of Nan getting up from her armchair. Then the shuffle of slippers on carpet before her silhouette appeared behind the sheer white curtain.

She slid the curtain aside and then opened the door and grabbed him and hugged him and cried.

"You two," she said, sobbing. She was wearing one of her brightly colored caftans. Pink and purple. Ben reached down to help Olive onto the veranda, and she squeezed between Nan and Ben, making a sandwich.

"Come on," Nan said. "Inside." She looked to the houses on either side and over the back fence, then slid the door shut and drew the curtain.

It was bright and warm inside, like always. Nan didn't like it when people turned lights off in her house.

"Still no word from Mum and Dad?" Ben asked.

"They called after you did. They're coming to get you. Soon, probably. I had to tell them."

Ben's stomach dropped. Nan squeezed them into her so tight that the three of them became one, like Ben and Olive could never go anywhere again.

"I knew you were alive," she said.

Ben felt the river rush through him for a moment.

"What happened to you?" Nan asked. "You both look so skinny and horrible! What have you been eating? And your hair's too short, Ben. What have they done to you?"

"Ben lost the money!" Olive said, dropping the words into the room.

Ben shot her a glare. Nan stopped and looked at him through her watery hazel eyes.

"What do you mean?" she asked.

"Mum and Dad, they—?" Ben began.

"I know what they did," she said.

Ben took a breath, ready to say what he had rehearsed, but he had been caught off guard by Olive.

"They kept some of the money in a bag," he said. "When we were in the bus shelter and got on the bus, there were tons of people around and I must have left it. We realized on the bus in the night but we were already so far down the coast and someone would have taken it, I know, and Dad's going to be so angry. I don't want him to come back here. Can you stop him coming back?"

He buried his face in Nan's shoulder so she could not look at him, and she put an arm around him. He continued babbling about how he didn't mean it, that he was stupid, that he had looked after the money all those days, carrying it up the river and then, at the end, when there was no danger, he had left it. Saliva and snot dripped from his face onto Nan's shoulder, and he wiped it off and rubbed it on his jeans.

"Don't worry," she said. She looked him in the eye. "Don't worry. Did you mean to leave it?"

Ben thought about the question, then shook his head.

"No, of course you didn't," she said. "Well, don't worry. It'll be okay. We'll work something out. At least you're back. You're much more precious than a bag full of money."

Ben wanted to believe that.

"Come," Nan said. "Come and eat. You must be starving."

They sat at the kitchen table, and she made them steaming-hot tea. Ben did not like tea but he drank it. Nan made him toast with Vegemite, and sugar toast for Olive. She cooked poached eggs with lots of salt and ketchup and she put the tall yellow cookie jar on the table in front of them along with glasses of milk. Olive did not eat much, and Ben felt sick after the eggs. He tried to keep eating to make Nan happy but the hole inside him was not as big as it used to be.

Ben told her everything about their ordeal. About the night the police came and the raft and the helicopter and the storm and the night he thought Olive might die and finding the cabin again and hitchhiking and the bus trip. Everything. Almost everything.

Nan listened and nodded and occasionally excused herself, going to the front window in the living room, peering through the curtains.

When Ben finished, Nan led Olive up the orange-carpeted hall to the bathroom. He heard the bath running and Nan and Olive chatting. He had always liked being at Nan's more than being at home. He took off his new shoes and peeled off the socks. They ripped at half-formed scabs on his feet.

"I'll make soup for lunch," Nan said, coming back into the kitchen.

Ben watched her chopping onions, thinking how easy food seemed now. Food had been so hard out there. Everything had been hard. He wanted to always remember.

She wiped her eyes with her wrist and looked at Ben in a funny way, scraping onions off the board into a pot.

"What?" Ben asked.

She took another onion and peeled it.

"I want to tell you something," she said.

Ben waited.

"They'll be here soon, but there's something you should know first."

Ben could feel the food and tea wrestling each other in his belly.

"It's about your grandfather."

Ben liked stories about Pop.

"He was a crook," she said, wiping onion tears. "He was a criminal, a scammer."

She chopped slowly now, looking to Ben for his reaction. "That's why he built that cabin. A place to hide out sometimes, till things cooled down."

Ben started to say something but he stopped. He was shocked, but he also felt as though he had somehow known this all his life. He thought of the stuff they had found in the cabin—the gun, the traps with tough steel jaws, and the safe. He thought of the story about the wolves in Pop's old notebook. He thought of his uncle arranging the car and giving Dad the bag.

"Is Uncle Chris dodgy too?" Ben asked.

"I don't know what your uncle Christopher is up to. A long time ago I decided it was best not to know."

"Do you think we have convict blood? Maybe we can't help it. The Silvers, I mean. Was Pop's dad a crook?"

"I don't know. Probably," she said. "Your grandfather nearly got me killed a thousand times. I hated it. And now your useless father is doing the same thing. Promise me something, Ben . . ."

He knew what she was going to say. She scraped another onion into the pot and pointed the knife at him.

"Don't turn out like your grandfather. Or your father."

Golden barked, and the gate in the back alley squealed open. Ben looked out the window, adrenaline churning through him.

"That's them," Nan said. "Come. Into my room. Let me deal with him."

She gave Ben a push in the back, ushering him down the darkened hall. She stopped at the bathroom. "C'mon, out you get," she said to Olive. "Whoops-a-daisy."

"I don't want to get out!" Olive protested. Ben heard Dad's footsteps on the back veranda. "Who is that? Is that Mummy?" Olive asked.

"Shhh," Nan said, wrapping her in a towel and guiding her down the hall to Ben, who was standing in the bedroom doorway. "I'll check, love. One thing at a time. Just let Nan go and speak to Mum and Dad and then you'll be able to give Mum a big hug, okay?"

Olive dripped on the carpet and shivered.

"Nice and quiet, you two. We'll surprise them." She winked at Olive.

"Is Ben going to get in big trouble for losing the money?" Olive asked.

"Shhh. That's a good girl. You get dressed." Nan pulled the door closed just as Ben heard the back door slide open.

"Hello?" It was Mum's voice.

"Coming," Nan said, slippers shuffling double time up the hall.

LAST STAND

The moment Ben heard his father's voice in the kitchen he heard another noise at the front of the house. A heavy knock on the front door.

Then footsteps. Fast. Down the hall. Bedroom door open. Mum. Short-cropped hair. Dark circles under her eyes.

Ben had planned to be strong, to not show any emotion. That was before he saw her face fall apart and the tears falling from her eyes. She looked as though she had been out in the wild too. She hugged them so tight Ben thought his ribs might break.

"I'm so sorry," she whispered, and it seemed to Ben that her whole body bucked with the crying and the grief and the happiness. He had never loved and hated a hug so much in his life.

"Let's go!" Dad said from the doorway, panicked.

Mum looked at him, still hugging Olive and Ben. "No."

The knock on the front door again.

"Don't say that. Come. Now." He grabbed her by the arm.

"Don't touch me!" she whispered, shaking her arm out of his grip. They stood, looking at one another for a few seconds.

Dad waved a hand toward the door. Mum walked into the hallway, one arm around Ben, one around Olive.

"Don't speak," Dad said as they walked up the hall.

"Where have you been?" Olive asked, ignoring him. "Where are we going?" and "Why are we going so fast?" and "Are you and Daddy in big trouble?"

They hurried through the living room. Nan stood at the front door, waiting to open it. Ben had a pretty good idea who might be on the other side. Nan waved them on, telling them to move it.

They went through the kitchen and out the back door.

"Where's the money?" Dad asked.

"Where are we going?" Ben said.

"Where is it?" Dad insisted.

Mum jumped off the veranda, holding Olive's hand. Ben followed them, then Dad, who slipped a piece of old rope through Golden's lead and tied her to a veranda post. He ran through the yard behind Ben. "Tell me where the money is," Dad said.

"I don't know," Ben replied.

They reached the back gate.

"Stop," Dad said in a fierce whisper. He looked back up at the house, toward the police officers' voices inside. He opened the back gate and edged an eye out into the alley. Footsteps, heavy, maybe a few hundred feet away. Dad pulled back into the yard, eyes watering. He was out of his depth, Ben knew.

Even more out of his depth than he was in day-to-day family life. Now he was in the Mariana Trench, the deepest part of the ocean, with his feet set in concrete.

"Come on!" Dad whispered, moving to the back of the old chicken coop. Gray, rotting timber and wire pocked with feathers from long-dead chickens.

Heavy-booted footsteps in the alley, close now.

"Squeeze in here."

There was a twelve-inch gap between the coop and the rear fence.

"We won't fit," Ben whispered. Dad squeezed in, grabbing Ben by the T-shirt and dragging him into the narrow space. Ben ate a mouthful of spiderwebs. Two or three police officers ran past in the alley, shadows flickering by in the gaps between fence railings.

"Ray. It's over," Mum whispered.

"Stop saying that. Get in here. Now."

"I don't want to," Olive complained.

"Shhh. Do it!" he whispered fiercely.

The back gate squealed open as Mum and Olive shuffled into the space behind the chicken coop. Olive first. Then Mum. The police officers entered Nan's yard to the sound of Golden's savage barking.

Ben listened, ears sharp.

"Are the police going to get us?" Olive asked quietly.

"Shhh," Dad said in an almost silent hiss.

"But *are* they?"

Cramped air, close breathing sounds. Things crawling on Ben's legs. He thought of Captain and Olive Thunderbolt. He wondered if any of the great bushrangers had ever hidden behind a chicken coop during their last stand.

Listening. Soon the police were talking to Nan at the back door. Nan losing her cool, telling them she's an old lady and to leave her alone.

"We know that they're here," said one of the officers in a voice that carried across the yard. "We'd appreciate it if you would . . ." Some of what he said was lost in Golden's barking. ". . . inspect the property."

Nan said something that Ben could not quite catch.

He had the same feeling as when the police had come to the front door looking for his parents. And when the four of them had crouched under the cabin, the night they ran. Now they were wolves behind the henhouse.

"Tell me where the damn money is," Dad whispered, his breathing measured.

Sweat trickled down Ben's temple. He thought of Pop's words scratched into the diary. Two wolves. Good and bad. Which wolf wins? The one you feed. He felt a deep tickle in his lungs and he wanted to cough. He tried to swallow it.

"He lost it," Olive offered.

Dad didn't say anything for a moment. Then, "Tell me that's not true."

Ben said nothing. He was more afraid of his father than he was of the police.

"That is all we have left now," Dad said. "They've frozen the rest of it. So please tell me that's not true."

"Why didn't you tell me Pop was a criminal?" Ben asked.

Their low voices were covered by Golden's relentless barking.

"Shut up with that," Dad whispered. "Tell me where it is."

Ben looked at him. Dad was sweating, shaking with fear.

A couple of officers were moving back down through the yard now.

Ben wondered what a bullet passing through his skin would feel like.

"I'm scared," Olive whispered. "I want to get out."

Mum hugged her close. "It's okay. It'll be okay," Mum whispered. "Ray?"

"Quiet," Dad said.

"What sort of people are we?" she asked.

"We'll be dead people if you don't shut up."

"If I want to speak I will speak, Ray," Mum said, raising her voice slightly. "We have our children back. It's over."

"I want to get out," Olive whispered. "This is not fun."

"We're going to get out," Mum said, rubbing Olive's shoulder.

"Shut. *Up*," Dad wheezed.

"No, I will not shut up. You shut up, robber man," Olive whispered back to him. "You wrecked everything."

Dad growled, as if he couldn't help himself. He reached past Ben's stomach and grabbed Olive's arm roughly. She started to cry.

"I'm done, Ray," Mum said. "You can't control me anymore."

"What?" he whispered, breathless.

Mum and Olive slid out from behind the chicken coop, Mum holding her arms in the air. "We're here," she announced, and the police moved in.

Ben squeezed out of the space and stood next to Olive, arms raised like in a movie. Mum stood slightly in front of them, protective. Ben turned, waiting for his father to join him, but all he saw were sneakers and legs. In those final seconds of their life on the run, without a single word, his dad mounted the back fence, silently vaulted into the alley, and disappeared. One clean, cunning movement.

Police quickly surrounded them, shouting, weapons drawn.

"Hands on heads. All of you! Go! Now!" An officer motioned to the middle of the yard.

"C'mon," Mum said. "Just stay with me."

Olive and Ben obeyed.

Another officer checked their hiding space behind the coop, but it was empty.

LIFE

"You keep runnin', you'll only go to jail tired."

Ben mumbled the words as he watched his clay characters run. Ben Silver, Sydney's toughest cop, and the zombie thief stopped halfway down the forest track and the screen flickered to black.

How is it going to end? He needed to know.

Ben rested Mum's laptop on his bed, stood, and picked up the barbell again. He did fifteen curls. It was months since he had done any work on his movie. Now he was trying to finish it for an English assignment. His old camera had been ruined in the river, but he'd managed to rescue the movie.

Ben flopped onto his bed and turned to an empty space a few pages from the end of his crusty brown leather notebook. The river had permanently disfigured it but he could still write on its crisp pages.

How will it end? Sometimes the hero realizes that the bad guy is inside him. Maybe Sydney's toughest cop is the zombie thief. Maybe Ben Silver, the cop, in some weird way, is trying to arrest himself, to save himself?

Dad and Pop, no matter where I go, are inside me, in my blood. Is it possible to outrun the blood you have inherited, to become somebody else?

Ben looked out the window, confused. Light and breeze flowed in. The relentless whir of traffic on the highway out front. His room at Nan's was smaller but brighter than in the old house. And he had to share with Olive, but that was okay.

Every day for the past three months, part of him had missed being in the wild. Not the storm or the hunger or the ants or eating leaves and grubs but the air and the openness and the lack of straight lines.

A knock at the door.

"Yeah?"

Nan popped her head in. "Your mum's leaving soon."

Ben followed Nan into the hall. Mum was in the bathroom doing her hair. She wore high heels, knee-length skirt, white shirt.

"Don't worry. You'll be fine, and you look gorgeous," Nan said.

"Thanks," Mum said, looking at herself, puffing her cheeks, exhaling stress in a long, thin stream.

She turned to Ben and gave him a look that was part-smile, part-apology. This had become her favorite look since everything happened. Ben did not like it much because he felt guilty too.

213

She kissed Ben on the cheek and brushed past, heading up the hallway. She grabbed her handbag from the hall stand near the front door, checking her hair again in the mirror.

"Wish me luck," she said.

"Luck," Ben said.

"Olive, love, your mum's going!" Nan called.

Olive ran in from the backyard. She was covered in dirt from her new veggie patch. "I want to come."

"Not today," Mum said.

"Where are you going again?" Olive asked.

Mum bent down to her level. "To court. You know that. Remember?"

"Why are you going to court again?"

This had been explained to Olive at least seven times.

"Because I did—"

"Because you did the wrong thing and you're going to face the consequences but then you're going to come home to us and everything will be okay forever," Olive finished.

Mum let a smile creep onto her lips. "Yes," she said. "That's it."

"Will Dad go to court?" she asked.

Mum squeezed her hands. "If they find him. Yes."

Mum stood. Nan and Ben hugged her, and she opened the front door.

Olive ran off into the backyard. "Love you!"

"It's still not too late for me to come with you," Nan said.

Mum shook her head. "I got myself in . . ."

She squeezed Ben's shoulder and looked into his eyes. "Whatever happens today . . . I know I've made bad decisions, but I will try to make it up to you. I will try to be better."

Ben held her gaze and then she turned away. She went down the steps and along the front path in the sunshine, looking confident even if she did not feel it. She climbed into her rusty red hatchback, started the car, put her blinker on, waved, and disappeared into the flow of traffic on the old highway.

"Is she really going to be okay?" Ben asked.

"I hope so," Nan said, wistful. She sat down on the stoop. "I'm going to sit awhile, wait for her."

"Won't she be gone for hours?"

"Possibly," she said.

Ben watched Nan for a moment and left the door open. He headed for the backyard, guilt and bad feelings weighing on him.

He went down the veranda steps. He had replaced the old ones with off-cuts from the lumberyard. It was a slightly wonky job, he thought, but at least they weren't rotting anymore. He walked down through the yard to the chicken coop. He picked up the shiny claw hammer Mum had bought him from the hardware store a few days earlier and he continued with the job of dismantling the chicken coop. James and Gus had come over and helped him with some of it. It was one of the first things he had vowed to do when they decided to live with Nan. He did not need to be reminded of that day.

Ben had already taken down the chicken wire, removed the roof and the sides. Now he knocked out sections of the frame, the rusty nails squealing as he prized them out of the timber and threw them on a pile.

As he worked he prayed for Mum. If she wasn't okay, if the ruling went against her, then Ben would have to reveal his secret. He knew that.

WITHIN THE WOODS

Ben flew steeply downhill, dodging rough, chocolate-brown tree trunks, heavy boots sinking into pine needles and rich black soil beneath. Sun lit him in sharp bursts as he thundered into the valley. The water-rush became ever louder as he descended, filling him up.

The river looked just as it had—sun hit the surface in patches, revealing muddy brown rocks beneath. Downstream was the waterfall that he and Olive had rafted over. And, soaring above him, the sheer sandstone wall on the opposite side of the river.

It was a year since he had been here. Just over. He had thought about this place every day, every minute for a year. Yesterday, Friday afternoon, all Ben could think of as he sat in his classroom was the cabin, the river, the trees, the feeling of this place. When the bell rang, he did not go to his locker. He walked to the front of the school where Mum was waiting in her old red hatchback. They drove till late, staying in a motel, then started out early.

He sank the shovel blade deep into the earth. He had buried it beneath the small pyramid-shaped boulder so that it might be safer. But he had done the deed at midnight and a lot can happen in a year. What if robbers had dug it up? He pushed hard, dug around the edges of the rock, and rolled it away. The soil was damp, easy to dig. He took off his jacket. It was early spring, lunchtime, and the air was hot and thick with the roar of cicadas.

Ben's shovel hit something hard. A *chink* of metal on tin. He dug and scraped till he could see the rusted green metal. He worked quickly to excavate his treasure, unearthing the trunk and pulling it up out of the ground.

He sat and looked at it for a minute, breathing heavily with the effort. He had waited this long. No rush now.

Open it or I will, he heard Olive say in his mind. But he sat there and looked at it for another minute or two before he slowly raised the lid to reveal the rotten gray nylon sports bag with the black handles. He smiled, the guilt of what he had done fluttering away for a moment.

Nine hundred and thirty-two thousand three hundred dollars.

He looked up the hill to see if Mum was there. She had promised to stay in the car in the clearing, to wait for him. He picked up a wad of cash, bruising the notes with the black soil from his fingers. Was it so bad for a kid in his situation to have put aside an insurance policy for him and his sister? He had told a lie. A big lie to his family, to the police. He had not lost the money at the bus shelter. But didn't he and Olive deserve the money after everything that had happened to them? Even now, after telling Mum and agreeing that they would give the money back, he wondered if they could keep just a little of it.

He held the money, felt the river flowing by and the cabin up the hill looming over him.

River, cabin, money.

Like grandfather, like father, like son. Was it really possible to escape what was written in his genes?

A great rush of wind blew through the gully, a wind that rustled the leaves on every tree and sent birds squawking in formation across the river and high up over the rock wall. Ben looked around and breathed it all in. He had missed this place. He felt mosquitoes take his blood and he pulled his boots off, digging his toes into the cool soil beneath.

He dropped the money back into the trunk and made his way down over the rocks to the river. He cupped his hands, dipped them in the water, splashed his face. It felt crisp and good, waking something inside him.

Ben thought of the night that he and Olive had run away from the cabin, from Mum and Dad, and of the deep hunger and pain and despair he had felt in those days coming up the river. He thought of Olive lying, half-dead, in the darkness just downstream from here. And he should have felt bad about the place, but he didn't. He knew now that everything bad would pass, and everything good would pass too. A never-ending stream. The river flowed on.

He splashed his face again and sat back on a rock, closing his eyes. He sat there for a long time, becoming so still he felt as though he had disappeared or had turned into one of the boulders he was surrounded by. Rocks that had been here forever. There was no "I'm me." "Me" seemed to disappear and this feeling was better than the money. Better than a trunk full of cash. This would have seemed ridiculous if it didn't feel so true.

His pulse was the pulse of the place, and he knew, deeply, as the moments passed, why he had come back. He felt something beyond money and family, beyond himself. And he knew that he would not run. He would give all the money back like he had promised Mum. He would leave it outside the police station in Kings Bay and walk away and never look back. The police would never know who left it there.

In that moment he knew how his story would end. This thought drove him up off the rock, and he staggered for a moment and his head felt light and all the colors were vivid and his head pulsed with hot blood. He steadied himself and climbed up the rocks and when he was almost to the top he saw a person standing beneath one of the pines.

At first Ben thought it was an illusion brought on by the sudden rush of blood to his head. It was a man, bearded and skinny, barefoot and wild-looking. He was holding the bag of money, the rotten bag with one broken black handle. He was holding it tucked under his arm just as Ben had done a year ago on his way upstream. Ben noticed that his left arm was heavily tattooed.

"Hello, Cop," the man said.

ONE WOLF

"Give me the bag," Ben said.

"Don't think so, Cop." Dad spat on the ground.

The word "Cop" made anger rise up in Ben, the opposite of the feeling he'd had down by the river.

"How long have you been here?" he asked.

Dad did not answer.

"Pretty stupid place to hide," Ben said.

"I've been living like an animal," Dad said. "Six months since I came back here and I've been sleeping so close to my money without knowing it."

"It's not your money."

"You stole it," Dad snapped.

"Not your money," Ben repeated.

"You're the same as me."

"I'm nothing like you."

"You, me, and my old man. We're all the same."

Ben did not say anything. He hated the truth of it. "I'm going to give the money back," he said. "And I'm going to tell the cops you've been here."

Dad laughed. "Is that before or after they stick you in prison for burying the money? Stupid boy."

He felt like a little kid again, like nothing he said or thought or did was worth anything. The difference was that Ben was almost as tall as Dad now, and after a year of lifting weights, better built. His father looked hungry, all sinewy arm muscles clinging to bone.

Ben moved toward him, and Dad scuttled back, an animal in dirty jeans and a filthy blue T-shirt.

Ben reached for the money, and Dad pushed him away, hard. Ben went down on his backside, then jumped back to his feet. He watched his father, the wild, crumpled figure of him, and he thought of Dad's sneakers disappearing over Nan's back fence while he and Mum and Olive were arrested.

"Y'know, Mum went to court and got off on probation. Uncle Chris got in big trouble for helping you. They almost put him away. But they said it was mostly your fault and they're chasing you. They want to lock you up."

Dad blinked.

"Mum's got a job, a good one that she actually likes. Nan and her have been paying off all your stupid debts from the wreckers."

"Yeah?" Dad said. "Why didn't you give 'em some of the cash you buried?"

Ben, angry now, moved quickly toward his father. When he came close Dad hit at his ears and his neck, awkward places, but Ben fended off most of it, head down, hands protecting himself. He grabbed the material of the bag and he pulled hard and the bag ripped but he took it from his father and he scrambled away and ran. He ran up the hill, through the trees. Dad gave chase but Ben was too quick.

He made it to the top of the rise and into the clearing and he saw Mum waiting there in the car. She opened the door and stood when she saw him.

"Ready to go?"

"Dad!" Ben said, panic tearing at him.

Dad loomed over the rise, limping toward the car like some zombie thief.

"Stay away!" Mum screamed, a mother bear protecting her cub, but Dad kept coming.

Ben made it to the passenger side, lifted the handle. He threw open the door, tossed the bag onto the floor, climbed inside. As he went to shut the door, Dad grabbed it, took Ben by the shoulder, pulled him up and out of the car, pressing him against the red metal, staring into his eyes. Dad was bearded, dirty, angry, saliva dripping between his hillbilly teeth, his fingers digging into Ben's skin.

"Leave him, Ray," Mum said, voice churning with panic. "Leave him!"

Dad swung a punch, but Ben dodged it and heard his father's knuckles crack against the door's rim. He grabbed Dad by the back of his dirty blue T-shirt, twisted it to make it tight, and dragged him away from the car. Dad scratched and clawed at Ben's arm, digging filthy fingernails into his flesh, but Ben did not care. He dragged him over the sand and dumped him at the cabin door.

"Give it to me," Dad said, sitting up and rubbing his neck where the T-shirt had dug in.

Ben backed off. Dad drew himself off the ground and moved quickly toward him again. Ben tried to move away but he was too slow and Dad wrestled him to the ground in front of the idling car, pinning him.

Ben had a flash of the last time the two of them had fought on this ground: when Dad had taken his notebook, mocked him, owned him, like some overgrown school bully. Ben had been an unfit, jam-doughnut-eating twelve-year-old then. Had not known who he was. Now, a year on, he was leaner, more muscular, while Dad had halved in size.

Ben twisted sharply and, in one motion, flipped his father over and sat on him, holding his wrists to the sand. Dad struggled and flopped but Ben held him. After a minute or two Dad stopped bucking and writhing. Ben stared into those red-rimmed, bloodshot eyes and he saw something he had not seen there before—defeat.

"I'm going to let you go, okay?"

Dad did not respond.

"Okay?"

Dad gave the slightest nod of his head. Ben let go of his father's skinny wrists. He stood and backed slowly toward the car.

"Ben, let's go," Mum said. "Get in."

Dad pushed up off the ground and stood like a lame dog. Ben continued to the car, wary, as Dad ran at him again with a growl. Ben raised his forearm in defense, and Dad bit him hard. Ben shoved him away.

There was blood on Ben's arm. His own or his father's, he did not know. "Go!" he shouted, like he was speaking to a vicious dog, and his father retreated. He recoiled and tripped and stood again at the cabin door.

"Ben!" Mum called. "Now. Leave him. It's over."

Ben held his arm and wiped the bite. It felt deep. He opened the passenger door. "I'm sorry," he said, and in his mind he heard his father say, *Don't say sorry. It's weak.*

He collapsed into the seat, slammed the door. The figure stood in the doorway of the cabin. Mum accelerated quickly across the clearing, and Dad chased. He beat on the front passenger window. He ran alongside the car and beat the window hard, leaving a smear of sweat and blood. He did the same to the rear passenger window, smashing on the glass. Dad clutched the edge of the window frame for a moment, but Mum yanked the wheel sideways and he fell away.

They drove. Ben checked the side mirror and saw Dad in the clearing. Standing, screaming at them, in front of Pop's cabin. Then the trees swallowed the car and they turned the corner and all Ben could see was dirt road, empty, ahead and behind. Mum turned another corner, powered up the hill, swerving around ruts and rocks. They drove on with Mum saying, "Are you okay? Are you okay?"

She flipped open the glove box, pulling three tissues from an old plastic packet.

"Put these on it."

"It's okay," Ben said.

She gave him a look, and Ben took the tissues.

They drove for ten minutes and eventually emerged from the gully and into the sunshine on the edge of the paved road. Mum brought the car to a stop, kicking up a cloud of dust.

Ben wound down the window. He could not hear the river but he heard the trees swirling gently around him, whispering, and he felt grounded again for a moment. He sat and breathed. Mum held his hand, and he clutched hers. She sobbed very quietly, and Ben dabbed at his bite mark, noticing the crookedness of the indent made by his father's teeth. For some reason he hoped that the bite would scar him, a permanent tattoo to remind him of where he had come from.

After a few minutes more, Mum put the car in gear and said, "We better go finish this."

Ben nodded, and they rolled forward. Mum turned right, toward Kings Bay. They coasted down the hill, windows open, wind roaring through them, feeling the enormity of what they were doing. Ben grabbed his old notebook out of the backpack on the floor of the car. Carved into the inside of the leather cover were the words *"Culpam Poena Premit Comes."* Ben had found the translation of it in a book—"Punishment follows closely on the heels of crime." It had proven true but it was almost too simple and neat for Ben now, too black-and-white.

On the first page of the notebook were the sums Pop had written in smudgy blue ink, probably for some dodgy deal gone wrong. Ben flicked to the back of the book and read that quote one last time.

Two wolves inside him. One good, one bad. A terrible battle.

Which one would he feed?

Which wolf would win?

Ben stared out the window, letting the world go by in a blur of trees and sky. He felt empty now, totally empty. In a good way. As though he had released his wolves from captivity. There was no "good" or "bad" wolf anymore, nothing to run from. For the moment, the terrible battle was done.

ACKNOWLEDGMENTS

The origin of the "two wolves" parable is often attributed as an old Cherokee tale, but this is disputed.

Thanks to Varuna Writers Centre. I wrote there for four glorious days and I carry that stillness with me now. Thanks to the Northern Rivers Writers Centre, where I wrote part of this manuscript. Thanks to the people who encouraged me to write this when I pitched it to them—kids and teens in schools, Sophie Hamley, John Boyne, Hux, and Luca. Thanks to Catherine Drayton for daring me to dig deeper and complete the journey.

I am indebted to Kimberley Bennett and Zoe Walton at Random House Australia and to Margaret Ferguson at Farrar Straus Giroux, who pushed me to rethink and rediscover. I have learned most of what I know about writing from the excellent editors I have worked with.

Thanks to my wife, Amber, for encouraging and inspiring my creative endeavors. Thanks to Jean Craighead George for writing *My Side of the Mountain* and to the other authors whose work dares me to be better and more honest.